CREED

ROCK HARD MOUNTAIN MEN

BOOK THREE

BY EVIE RILEY

CREED

ROCK HARD MOUNTAIN MEN

BOOK THREE

COPYRIGHT © 2025

EVIE RILEY

ISBN: 978-1-77357-751-7

978-1-77357-752-4

PUBLISHED BY NAUGHTY NIGHTS PRESS LLC

COVER ART BY CDG COVER DESIGNS

CHAPTER ONE

Creed

I AWOKE IN a panic. Sweat dripped over my heated skin, quickly cooling in the night air and summoning goosebumps from my flesh. It felt like every hair on my body was standing on end.

Someone was watching me.

Grabbing the knife hidden under my pillow, I threw it with all the force I could muster while sitting up in bed.

The knife cut the air with an audible whistle. Even without seeing it, I could tell it was a good throw.

However, instead of the damp sound of metal piercing flesh that I expected, there was a sharp crack of something breaking instead.

Reaching out blindly in the dark, I groped for the light sitting by the bed. Everything in the room was new and unfamiliar, and I knocked the shade clear off the lamp before I managed to turn it on.

The glow of the now bare bulb illuminated the walls of Brody's guest room around me. It was small but neatly furnished. He'd put a lot of care into designing everything, just like he had the rest of the house he'd built for himself.

A mirror hung on the wall across from me. The once spotless surface was now marred with spiderweb cracks, spreading out from my knife that pierced it right through the center.

Right between the reflection of my own

eyes.

"Damn," I muttered as I ran a hand through my short hair, wincing at how sweaty it felt. "Not again."

I'd hung that mirror there to hide yesterday's knife mark, which I'd left after the previous night's bad dream. If this kept up, I was going to have to explain to Brody why I kept making holes in his house.

He'd understand. Brody, Magnus, and I had all fought on the frontlines together. We all understood the nightmares that came with such experiences.

Still, I'd prefer to avoid the conversation entirely.

Sighing again when I realized it wasn't just my hair that was sweaty, but my whole body as well, I rose from the bed to take a shower.

Brody had done a good job designing the place. Even the guest bathroom had ample space. My elbows didn't even touch the walls of the shower no matter how I moved. It was practically five-star luxury after the Spartan military life I'd been living.

Too bad I couldn't enjoy it.

After my shower, I checked the clock. It was only a few hours until dawn. Certain that I wasn't going to get any more sleep, I went downstairs to make myself a cup of coffee. That alone took a half hour of my time as I struggled to figure out Brody's fancy coffee machine. I could bushwack my way through wild terrain, and fly a chopper through hostile airspace, but figuring out the exact sequence of buttons and levers had had to push just to make myself a drink was worse than diffusing a bomb.

Which I'd also done before. Only once, but once was enough.

I sat on the couch by the window without turning on any lights, content to watch the night sky.

CREED

The sound of footsteps in the dark put me on edge. My hand drifted to the knife on my belt, which never left my side. However, a moment later, instead of the attacker I expected, I was instead greeted with the sight of a dog approaching me. Brody and Magnus had told me about the dogs they adopted, and I'd seen them a few times through videocalls, but never met the creatures in person until a few days ago. Luckily, those videocalls were enough for them to recognize my voice, so the dogs accepted me into their territory easily. I would have hated to be at odds with Brody and Magnus's new pets.

The Pitbull that approached me now, which I thought was named Indigo, hopped up onto the couch next to me and laid down with a great sigh, as if it had just run a marathon. Its wide head pressed right against my leg, so close that I could feel every movement when it breathed.

Nothing happened for a moment, but then the dog huffed and shifted position to put its head right in my lap. Large eyes stared up at me with a look that I swore seemed like it was scolding me for something.

I met the creature's gaze, not sure what to do. I'd never really been an animal person. The only pet I'd ever had was the cat my family had when I was a kid. The little beast hadn't liked me and clawed at me whenever I came near it.

The dog let out another huff, then butted my hand with its head.

Finally picking up the cue, I started stroking its head. The fur was very short, but also softer than expected. Its silver-blue fur had an almost metallic sheen, but the texture made me think of velvet rather than steel.

I'd heard that dogs were therapeutic. It had never made much sense to me before.

What therapy could a creature that

couldn't even talk really offer?

Now, however, I started to understand. There was a comfort to be found in the presence of a dog that a human couldn't provide. No matter how much I cared about Brody and Magnus, if they had been the ones to find me down here in the middle of the night, they would have had questions that I would have had to answer. With a dog, no conversation was necessary. I could just enjoy the presence of another living creature without having to explain the nightmares that kept me awake, or the multiple knife marks that littered my bedroom walls.

I wouldn't have known how to explain even if the dog could ask.

The dawn eventually came, but still neither Brody nor Magnus appeared.

I didn't see another living soul until nearly nine in the morning.

"Nice to see you among the living," I said when Brody stepped downstairs.

His hair was still mussed from sleep, and his shirt wasn't buttoned, so it hung open. Red marks covered his chest. They blended in with his equally red chest hair, so they were hard to see, but they definitely hadn't been there the day before.

I turned my gaze away from the marks, trying to ignore where they must have come from.

Brody didn't even hesitate as he made himself a drink from the coffee machine. "This is a perfectly normal time to wake up. Your perception is just skewed because you're too used to military time."

I pretended to take a sip from my empty coffee mug to make it look like I hadn't been sitting there that long.

"It wasn't that long ago that you were living on military time as well. It's been less than a year since you retired. Do old habits really die so quickly?"

Brody raised an eyebrow at me over

the rim of his mug as he took a sip of his own fresh coffee.

"Are you really judging me for living like a civilian?" he asked as he started preparing breakfast.

With a pang of guilt, I realized that was exactly what I was doing. Some part of me had expected everything to stay the same, even after we retired. Same morning routine, same division of labor, same strict schedule.

It was a foolish thought. I should have realized that leaving the military behind meant more than just a change of location.

My guilt intensified as I watched Brody cook. I'd already been awake for hours. I could have prepared food for everyone, but the thought hadn't even crossed my mind.

There was no helping it now. I'd just have to find another way to make myself useful.

"What's the plan for today?" I asked when it seemed like Brody was almost done cooking.

"There's some things we need to take care of," he said without looking away from whatever he was stirring in a skillet. "But let's wait for the others to get here to discuss it."

The fact that he'd said "others" instead of "Magnus" was just dawning on me when someone descended the stairs.

The man that stepped into view was a stranger.

Brody had introduced him to me. I knew his name was Ellis Beckham and that he apparently lived here now, but in my mind he was still just a stranger that I didn't know.

At almost the same time, the front door opened, and Magnus entered the house with an enthusiastic greeting. Another stranger walked at his side as well. A man named Trent, who I didn't know any more than I knew Ellis.

Right. Brody and Magnus had partners now.

That was... going to take some getting used to.

I'd always known that Brody and Magnus were gay. Technically, I was as well, but it was a fact that I'd never been comfortable enough to look at very closely.

'Don't ask, don't tell' may have ended years ago but I was quite comfortable keeping such things out of sight and out of mind. It was just one more complication that I didn't need.

Now, however, reality was blatantly staring me in the face as I was invited to the breakfast table.

Conversation passed between the four of them easily. For Magnus and Brody this wasn't surprising, but the new additions—Ellis and Trent—also joined in easily. They seemed as comfortable as if they were in their own home.

Because they were home.

Somehow, while being introduced to these other two men, I'd completely glossed over the fact that they lived here.

At least, I think that was the case. I remembered Magnus saying something about Trent having his own place in town, but that might have been a business and not a home. So much had been thrown at me at once when I arrived, I'd missed some of the explanation.

No matter what, even if this new pair didn't truly live here, this place was definitely as comfortable to them as a home.

I'd helped buy the property, and owned a third of the land, but it wasn't my home. I was the stranger here. The new arrival that didn't fit.

"Hey, Creed. You okay?"

Magnus's question snapped me out of the daze I'd fallen into. I realized I'd been staring at my own plate for a while, not even seeing the food in front of me. I hadn't even picked up my fork to start eating, which must have looked odd when the others were at least halfway done with their own meals.

Clearing my throat, I reached for my coffee mug, which had been refilled at some point. "Yeah. I'm fine. Um... Brody, didn't you say there was something we needed to talk about?"

Brody sat at the head of the table like he was the father at a cliché thanksgiving dinner scene. Setting his cutlery aside, he sat in silence for a moment with a pensive look on his face before speaking up. "In case anyone hasn't noticed... there's a giant hole in the middle of our property."

Magnus snorted as he held back an ugly laugh. "No kidding. I'm lucky to have any of my garden left, and my plans for a greenhouse are definitely fucked. What about it."

"Well..." Lacing his fingers together, Brody propped his chin on top of his hands. "We're going to need to fix it. Which is going to cost money. A lot more money than we had planned."

As everyone else cringed and muttered under their breath, I quickly ran a few numbers through my head.

When we'd bought this property and made our construction plans, we'd obviously saved extra for contingencies, but we hadn't planned for a literal cave-in. I didn't know exactly how much it would take to fix such a thing, but I could estimate a few numbers, and it didn't look good. We'd probably be able to fix that house-sized hole in the ground, but it wouldn't leave us money for anything else.

"I've called my boss at the logging company," Brody continued, his breakfast now completely forgotten. "He's allowed me to pick up a few more shifts, but that's not going to cut it. So, any ideas?"

Magnus leaned back in his chair until the wood creaked from the strain of his weight. "I could enter a few more cage fights. It's good money, but it's not reliable enough for us to count on."

"What about offering training?" Trent suggested.

Magnus dropped back onto all four legs of his chair with a heavy thud. "What do you mean?"

For such a large man, Trent looked surprisingly boyish when he blushed. "Well, when I was watching your last fight, I heard a lot of people talking about how skilled you were in the ring, and how they'd give anything to know your secret. I bet there'd be plenty of people willing to pay you to train them. I know firsthand how valuable a good trainer can be. When I first started competitive weightlifting, I went through three different trainers before I found a decent one, and let me tell you, they weren't cheap."

I knew about Magnus's moonlighting work as a cage fighter, but I was surprised to hear that Trent had attended his fights. The man didn't look like the type who would enjoy violence, even the recreational kind. It just went to show how much I didn't know about Magnus or Brody's partners.

Trent's suggestion was a good idea. I could picture it. Out of the three of us, Magnus had always been the most personable, but he also didn't take any bullshit. It could be a good job for him if he could get enough clientele, and from the sounds of it, he already had some interested people.

"Also, I've been thinking," Trent continued, tapping his fork against his plate in a way that set my teeth on edge. "For my antique business, I do most of my sales online these days. I'd still keep the store for posterity's sake, maybe open it a couple days a week, but there's no reason for me to keep the apartment above the shop. I basically live here now, anyway, so I might as well rent it out to earn some more income."

So, he was an antique dealer and a competitive weightlifter. Those seemed like an odd combination, and I wondered how he'd gotten involved with Magnus in the first place. I hadn't heard much about how they met. While I was still serving overseas, it hadn't mattered. Magnus's blooming relationship had just been a story from a life that was happening on the other side of the world.

Now, it was going to be a part of my everyday life, and I was curious. Last I knew, Magnus still tripped over himself every time he tried to talk to someone that he found attractive, and I'd half expected him to stay single forever.

Magnus placed a hand on Trent's leg, squeezing his thigh in a gesture that was so intimate I had to look away.

"Hey, Trent, we aren't asking you for money. We bought this property. Taking care of it is our responsibility."

Trent was already shaking his head, though he never tried to remove Magnus's hand. "No. I basically live here already, and if I rent my apartment, then your home really will become mine as well. That means, I also need to take care of it."

"I agree," Ellis said suddenly. "He shrank in his seat a bit when all eyes turned toward him but kept talking anyway. "Brody, you... you said I could stay with you, but I can't just be a freeloader. I'm not sure what I can offer, but now that I've got my identity back, I can at least start looking for a part-time job in town."

Got his identity back?

There was a story there that I wasn't aware of. I remembered Brody saying something about Ellis suffering amnesia not long ago.

Maybe it had to do with that?

I'd have to ask later.

The conversation turned toward everyone's plans for the day. Trent was going to drive into town to check on his shop and start getting his apartment ready to rent, and Ellis asked to go along with him so he could start looking for work. Meanwhile, Brody insisted that he and Magnus needed to work on the hole in the middle of the property. We didn't have the means to fix it, yet, but the collapsed ground at least needed to be shored up to ensure nothing else collapsed.

No one made any suggestions about what I should do. At first, I felt insulted, like I'd been purposely excluded from the conversation. Then, however, I realized I wouldn't have known what to say if I was part of the conversation, and I felt relieved that I'd been left out of it.

I'd dumped all my savings into buying this property, just like Magnus and Brody had.

I was just as committed as them, but what else could I do?

Now that I'd retired from the military, what job could I do to earn money?

Infiltrating enemy territory wasn't exactly a transferable skill to civilian life. Brody and Magnus both had interests outside of their military career that they'd managed to take advantage of, but I wasn't the same. My priority had always been survival. I could ensure that every member of my unit got to their destination safely, but survival wasn't a job. There was no way to make money just by "surviving".

After breakfast—which I'd barely touched—I offered to help Brody and Magnus. I knew nothing of construction. That was Brody's area of expertise. Even Magnus, with his interest in plants, understood at least a little about how the soil worked. I, on the other hand, was completely out of my depth, and had to rely on the others for instruction. I could, at least, follow instructions.

Brody directed Magnus and I to remove as much rubble as possible from the pit in the middle of the property while he inspected the old foundation holding up the tunnel. We would need to build new supports, eventually, but before that, we would first need to clear out a space to work.

With some old timber plants, Magnus and I cobbled together a makeshift ramp we could use to carry the broken earth and stone out of the pit. Many of the pieces were too big for one person to lift, so we had to work together.

I kept silent through most of it, mulling over my thoughts as my body worked on autopilot. Magnus and Brody were used to this and didn't question my silence. In fact, Magnus looked more shocked when I finally spoke up.

"So, Mag," I said suddenly after the third load of debris we carried up the ramp. "How did you and Trent meet? You never told me much about that."

I may not have any idea what to do with myself, but if I was going to be living with these two new strangers, then I should at least learn more about them.

Magnus's surprise over my unexpected question was quickly replaced by excitement as he gushed about his newfound partner. Apparently, they'd met because of the body that Magnus discovered, which seemed like a morbid start to a relationship, but I just nodded along as he told me about their first meeting. I knew nothing about healthy relationships. The longest romantic relationship I'd ever maintained only lasted a few weeks. So long as Magnus was happy, then I saw no reason to complain.

Magnus and Brody were happy here. That was probably the part I struggled with the most. The two of them had settled down easily, building their homes, and almost immediately finding luck in their love lives. It was like happiness had just been handed to them on a silver platter, and I had no idea how they did it.

Could I be happy here as well?

When retiring and buying a property together had just been a dream, I thought I could be happy with such a life. Now that it was my reality, however, I wasn't sure.

The day passed by in a whirlwind of hard work. Trent and Ellis returned just before sundown, and we all piled around the dinner table for another shared meal. Ignoring the fact that we were five burly men, it was like something straight out of a sitcom or a Hallmark movie, where the family all sits down together at the dinner table to discuss their day. Everyone was smiling and joking. They asked Ellis if he'd had any luck applying for jobs and inquired about the process it would take for Trent to rent his apartment.

It should have been a happy scene.

So, why did it set my teeth on edge?

Maybe there was something wrong with me.

I barely said two words during dinner, thankful for my already stoic personality. No one questioned my silence, and other than a few sidelong glances from Brody and Magnus, I was mostly left alone as if I was nothing more than another part of the decoration.

Hours later, I found myself lying on my bed, staring up at the dark ceiling of the guestroom. I was exhausted after a day of hard labor, but my thoughts were too chaotic to sleep.

"Alcohol," I eventually declared aloud after checking the clock to see that it was nearly midnight. "Maybe alcohol will solve my problem."

Getting drunk would at least be better than lying awake all night.

Leaving the guest bedroom behind, I headed down to the kitchen without turning on any lights. If I knew Brody, which I did, then there would be at least one bottle of quality whiskey or scotch hidden somewhere in his pantry.

As I passed near the master bedroom, I heard strange sounds coming through the door. I only paused for a moment to listen, before realizing the sounds were of an intimate nature, and quickly hurried on my way.

The alcohol wasn't even hidden. It was displayed proudly on a custom wine rack where anyone could take it. Not even bothering to pour myself a drink, I grabbed an entire bottle of whiskey and turned to head back to my room. Then I realized that meant passing by the master bedroom again.

Not wanting to hear any more of Brody's private life, I headed for the porch instead.

The night was overcast. I could still see the general outline of the moon, but it was hazy and ill-defined. Occasional stars peeked through gaps in the clouds, gone almost as soon as they appeared.

No one, not even the night sky, could judge me as I leaned back and drank straight from the bottle in my hand.

Sip by sip, the night slowly crept by. I couldn't see enough of the bottle to know how much I'd drunk, but I could feel the alcohol heating my veins, so I knew it must have been a substantial amount. Just as I was considering if I should go back inside and try to sleep again, my drunken daze was interrupted by the sound of my phone ringing. I jumped, having completely forgotten that I'd brought the thing outside with me, and nearly dropped the bottle.

Who was calling me in the middle of the night?

I fumbled with the phone for a moment before finally looking at the screen. I recognized the number and immediately felt myself relax.

Hitting the answer button, I put the call on speaker so I wouldn't have to worry about clumsily holding it up to my ear.

"Kayden? Why are you calling me so late?"

"Creed," the familiar voice of my oldest friend answered. "Been awhile since I talked to you. I was just... wait. What do you mean late? Isn't it the middle of the day where you are?"

Oh, right. I hadn't told Kayden about my earlier retirement. As far as he knew, I was still serving overseas.

Well, at least that explained the odd time for the call.

"Actually, I'm back stateside."

"What? Really?"

His voice was earnest, reminding me of the innocent excitement of childhood. Even now that we were in our forties, Kayden had never lost his upbeat personality.

"Yeah," I said, grimacing when I heard how somber I sounded compared to him. "It's... complicated. Some stuff happened, but I got to retire a few months early."

"Stuff?" Kayden repeated. Just that one word, and I knew he'd already seen right through me.

We'd grown up as childhood friends, but life had taken us in different directions. Now, our friendship mostly consisted of phone calls and occasional video chats. I hadn't actually seen the man face to face in years, yet he still had the uncanny ability to read me better than anyone.

"I take it you don't want to talk about

this 'stuff', so I'll just ask, are you okay?"

"Yeah, I'm fine," I said, and immediately grimaced. I'd answered too quickly, and my voice was too high. There was no way Kayden wouldn't notice.

"Are you sure you're okay?" Kayden insisted.

Yep, he'd noticed.

The word "yes" was on the tip of my tongue. I'd already curled my lips around the syllable, but before I could breathe life into the word, I hesitated.

"No." The admission slipped out of me like a prisoner making its escape from a poorly locked cell. Just two little letters, but once I said them out loud, I couldn't seem to stop talking.

"Retirement isn't what I expected. I don't know what I expected, but it's not... Brody and Magnus have partners now, which is great for them, but also odd. We need money, so I should get a job, but I have no idea what to do. I just don't seem to... fit anywhere."

"I see," Kayden said, and even through the phone I could hear the wide-eyed expression he must be wearing as he listened to my sudden rambling. "That sounds like a lot. So, your friends, Magnus and Brody, you said they have... partners now?"

Sighing, I set the half empty bottle of whiskey down on the floor by my feet and let my head fall against the back of my chair. "Yeah. Don't get me wrong, Ellis and Trent seem great, and Mangus and Brody are both happy, but it's just odd. The dynamic has changed, and I don't know how to react."

There was a pause on the other end of the line, which was unusual. Kayden almost always knew what to say. As a travel writer, words were his livelihood.

The silence didn't last too long, but when Kayden did find his voice again, it was more hesitant than normal. "Maybe I misheard, but your friends are gay?"

Hearing the word "gay" out loud caused my brain to stall for a second. I never really spoke about it, not even with Magnus and Brody. It was just one of those unspoken truths that hung between us. People either already knew, or they didn't, and I never bothered to correct them either way.

Maybe it was time to change that.

So many other things about my life were already changing, what difference would one more change make?

"Yeah. They are."

I instinctively reached for the whiskey bottle again, but then stopped myself.

"And you're... okay with that?"

I snorted directly into the phone.

"I'd be a hypocrite if I wasn't."

There. I'd admitted it. Sort of. Sure, I hadn't directly used the word "gay," but the meaning was still clear. That had to count for something.

This time there was an even longer pause on the other end of the line. If it weren't for the fact that I could hear the soft sound of a television playing in the background of Kayden's call, I would have thought the line disconnected.

"I see." His voice was smaller than I'd ever heard it, like the squeak of a distraught mouse. Before I could think too much of it, however, he cleared his throat, and everything suddenly snapped back to normal. "That's gotta be a hard adjustment, but just give it time. I'm sure it'll get better. Did you also say something about needing money?"

"Oh, yeah. That's a long story."

Stretching out my legs, I crossed my ankles over each other as I settled in to recite everything that had happened so far, leading up to the giant hole that now stood in the center of our property and needed to be fixed.

By the end of it, I wasn't sure if I'd

made any sense, but Kayden's voice had returned to its usual upbeat tone.

"You know, if you need a job, I might be able to help with that. I've been traveling all over the world writing about different places, but my publisher has suggested that I focus on more domestic locations to balance things out. I hadn't planned anything yet, but a rustic camping trip through the mountains would be a great option. I could hire you as my guide, if you wanted."

I sat up quickly in my chair, accidentally kicking the whiskey bottle and spilling its contents across the porch. "Would that really work?"

"Of course it would work. You can make some quick cash. I can keep my publisher happy. Everybody wins."

I thought about the offer for a moment, weighing the pros and cons, but it was all in vain. I already knew I was going to accept. Guiding Kayden through the mountains was one of the only ways I could think of to earn money doing something I was good at.

Plus, it would be a great excuse to get some distance from Magnus and Brody. It felt horrible to admit such a thing, especially since I'd only just arrived, but I needed some time away from them to get my head on straight and adjust to our new situation.

"All right," I agreed when there was no reason for me to delay any longer. "We'll set up the details tomorrow. It's late right now, and I'm a bit too drunk."

I heard movement on the other end of the line, but it wasn't enough to tell what Kayden was doing.

"Oh, yeah. It is late. You should totally go to bed. And sober up. I'll talk to you later."

After my own goodbye, the line went dead. I shoved the phone back into my pocket and fetched the whiskey bottle that had rolled across the porch. Only a swallow of liquid remained in the bottle, the rest of it either already in my stomach, or spilled across the porch floorboards.

There was no point in returning such a little amount back to Brody's shelves. Raising the bottle to the sky, I toasted the moon where it was still hidden behind the clouds.

"Well, there's one problem solved. Maybe now I can finally get a few hours of peaceful sleep."

I downed the last bit of whiskey in one go.

It was even later than I thought when I returned to my room. As I passed the master bedroom, everything was silent. No passionate noises greeted me from the other side of the door, and I crossed the hall toward my own bedroom with a new spring in my step.

CHAPTER TWO

Kayden

"OH, FUCK," I said as I paced restlessly back and forth across the room. "Oh, fuck. Oh, fuck. Oh, fuck."

These were the only words that I'd been able to utter for the last fifteen minutes, but there was so much more than I wanted to scream about.

Creed was gay.

How had I not known this?

I'd been friends with Creed since we were kids. We went to middle school and high school together. We'd talked to each other at least every couple of days for most of our lives.

How had the topic of sexuality never come up before?

Forcing myself to stop pacing, I stood in the middle of my studio apartment and took a deep breath.

The answer was simple. The topic of sexuality had never come up because I avoided it at all costs.

But still, hearing Creed confirm that he was actually gay hit me like a slap to the face.

I'd been in love with him since we were kids. He was my first crush, and the reason I became a travel writer in the first place.

When he left for the military right out of high school, I started traveling to keep myself occupied and to stop myself from doing anything foolish, like running after him. That had eventually led to my career writing about all the places I'd visited.

For thirty years I'd carried this flame, snuffing it down until it was nothing more than a barely glowing ember, but still never able to extinguish it.

What would I have done all those years ago if I knew I had a chance?

"No," I reminded myself out loud as I started pacing again. "Don't be stupid. Just because he's gay doesn't automatically mean he'd be interested in you. Besides, he's already living with two other men. He's building a home with them. It's clear where he wants to be."

Although, apparently those other men, Brody and Magnus, had found their own partners. So, maybe...

No.

I cut that thought off immediately. I couldn't judge just based on that. For all I knew, they could have some kind of open relationship. I needed to play it cool and keep my thoughts and feelings to myself.

While camping.

With Creed.

Out in the woods, alone, just the two of us.

Probably sharing a tent.

"Oh, fuck," I shouted again as I dived for my phone and quickly dialed my editor's number.

It took several rings before the other end of the line picked up.

"Kayden, its two in the morning? What the fuck do you want?"

I checked the clock and flinched. Oops. She was right. It was the early hours of the morning. Traveling as much as I did, I lived in a constant state of jetlag, so my sense of time was permanently skewed.

"Oh, sorry, Helen. I didn't realize the time."

She grumbled, but I could hear her getting out of bed. Helen had been my editor for several years, and by now, she was used to my bad sense of time.

Although, even for her, two in the morning was probably pushing it.

"Well, I'm awake now. So, what do you want?"

"You know how we were just talking about where I was going to go for my next piece?"

On the other end of the line, I heard Helen shuffling through a few pages. "Yeah. We had it narrowed down to either the Himalayas, or the Andes mountains."

"Well, I was thinking I could do something a little closer to home this time."

"Closer to home?"

Her voice was completely deadpan. I couldn't tell what she thought of the idea, so I valiantly pressed on.

"Yeah, you know. Like, exotic mountains are great, but for people who want to travel on a budget, we've got plenty of beautiful mountains right here at home."

More paper rustling.

"We do have a collection of domestic travel articles that we've been putting together, but I thought you specifically requested to travel overseas. If I remember your exact words were 'If I'm going to go through the effort of traveling somewhere, it's got to be some place worth the effort'. What's changed?"

The true explanation, that my old childhood crush had just come out of the closet to me and now I was looking for any excuse to go see him, would have made me sound like a crazy person. Instead, I merely shrugged and tried to play it casual.

"I guess it's true what they say. Absence makes the heart grow fonder. All these years traveling to foreign places has given me a new perspective on my home country, and I'd like a chance to explore it better."

"Mmhm." She didn't sound convinced.

"Well, whatever your reason, I guess we can make it work. But once you commit to this, you can't change your mind at the last minute and decide you want to go somewhere else. So, I'll ask you one more time. Are you sure?"

Was I sure?

Absolutely not. But I was doing it anyway.

"Of course," I said. "When am I ever not sure?"

"Do I need to remind you about the llama incident?"

Of course she would bring that up. To make a long story short, I'd basically tried to pet a llama when I shouldn't have, and nearly lost a finger for my troubles. There was a three-inch-long scar running down the side of my hand as a permanent reminder.

"This isn't going to be anything like the llama incident."

"And what makes you so sure?"

"Well, for one, there definitely won't be any llamas involved."

I heard her sigh on the other end of the line, and if I had to guess, she was probably rolling her eyes at me as well.

"Fine. Give me the details and I'll file the request for your next project."

I immediately started to tell her about my plan, but she cut me off before I could get two words out.

"Tomorrow. It's the middle of the night and I'm not subjecting myself to any more of your insanity than I have to. Good night."

I laughed at her aggrieved tone, and kept going even after the line went dead.

That was that. Once Helen put in the request there was no going back. She was a great editor, but she was also a hard-ass who refused to bend for anyone. It helped to keep me on target, and now her efficiency was going to ensure that I couldn't chicken out from meeting with

CREED

Creed.

It was going to be the first time in years I saw the man face to face. Although I considered him a friend, I usually avoided being around him for fear of losing control and doing something I would regret.

Now, with a new hope rekindled in my heart, I was planning on isolating myself in the mountains with him. Even I could recognize that it was a recipe for disaster, and probably just going to result in getting my heart broken, but I had to at least try. I'd regret it the rest of my life if I didn't.

"Fuck," I groaned one last time as I collapsed onto my couch. "These next few weeks are going to be... interesting."

I must be a masochist. That was the only explanation for why I insisted on torturing myself.

***

A week later, I was packed up and driving out to a town called Emberwood to meet Creed. It took longer than I expected. My rental car was uncomfortable to drive in the way that all unfamiliar cars are. Plus, the mountain back roads were particularly confusing, and I got lost three times on the way.

"This can't be right," I muttered as I slowly guided my car down the dirt road. "This is just... trees. This is a forest. I haven't passed another building for miles. I don't think I'm even in Emberwood anymore."

The sun was going to set soon. There were no streetlights out on these back roads. For now, there was still enough light to see by, but once the sun went down it was going to get really dark.

I was just debating if I should turn around and find a place to stay back in town for the night, when a small turnoff with a sign next to it caught my eye.

CREED

The numbers on the sign matched the address Creed had given me. I had no idea if I was even on the right road, but it was the only lead I had.

The road I turned onto was even more obscure than the one I left behind. It barely even counted as a road, more like a footpath. If it weren't for the sign of fresh tire tracks, I would have turned around. Assuming I even could turn around on the narrow road on the edge of the mountain, that is.

It took another five minutes of driving before the endless tunnel of trees finally opened onto level land.

I immediately knew I was in the right place. Everything was exactly as Creed had described. There were two log cabin style houses, that apparently his friend Brody had built by hand, along with several other structures including a workshop, chicken coop, and a few other buildings I didn't know the purpose for.

One of the houses was surrounded by an extensive garden, right next to a huge pit in the ground. Reflective orange tape had been strung around the hole, warning people to stay away from it.

My curiosity was piqued. Creed had told me the story of the hidden tunnel under their property that had collapsed, but I would have to find an opportunity to see if for myself.

Caution tape be damned. I had never let a "keep out" sign prevent me from going where I wanted to.

I pulled my car up next to several rugged trucks on a flat gravel area. There were a few beams framing the gravel, like they'd started laying out the base for a garage but got distracted almost as soon as they started and now there was just the promise of a structure left behind.

The trucks were huge and made my four-door sedan look like a compact car. Remembering the harrowing drive to get out here, I could understand why they needed such impressive machinery. I would have to remember to rent a truck if I ever came out here again.

I was just stepping out of the car when Creed's familiar voice greeted me.

"Kayden. You made it."

With my back still turned to him, I hesitated. This was the point of no return. Right now, I could still jump back in my car and make my escape. It would probably mean an end to my friendship with Creed, but it was an option. Once I turned around and faced him, I'd be stuck. There was no way I'd be able to bring myself to leave, even if I wanted to.

Clenching my fists in front of me so Creed wouldn't see them, I put a big smile on my face and turned around to face him.

"Creed, it's been a long time," I greeted him, trying not to show my surprise at his proximity. The man was completely silent when he walked. He was already just a few feet away and I hadn't heard him approach at all.

When we were younger, I would have run up and hugged him, but those kinds of gestures stopped on my fifteenth birthday, when I first realized the extent of my feelings for him. From then on, whenever I wanted to greet him, I always just slung an arm over his shoulder, careful to keep our bodies angled away from each other.

Now, I didn't even have the right for that much.

How were you supposed to greet someone that you hadn't seen in person for years?

A handshake was too formal and didn't adequately express how happy I was to see him, but anything else felt too intimate.

In the end, I settled for a hearty slap on the shoulder.

CREED

"It's a miracle I got here at all. The place was hard to find. I got lost three times on the way here."

He was bulkier than I remembered. A lot of his size came from muscle, which I could feel through his clothing when I touched his shoulder. The man was practically made from stone. Yet, there was also some softness around his stomach that hadn't been there when we were younger. It looked good on him. When we were teenagers, there had been an unpleasant leanness to him, as if he had to keep himself in fighting shape at all times and could never relax. I'd been afraid that the military would exacerbate this, honing an already sharp blade until it broke, but it seemed like a life of service had provided him some comfort as well.

"You look good, man. Are you settling into your retirement?"

We'd spoken over the phone about how out of sorts he felt as he tried to find his place in civilian life, but that had been a week ago. Maybe he'd made some progress since then.

Creed merely answered with a shrug, which meant he wasn't willing to talk about it.

His dark eyes then raked over me.

"You've gained weight."

Anyone else would have been offended by this statement. Creed's lack of tact had driven many people away from him in the past.

However, when I heard him, I immediately started laughing as I was flooded with a sense of relief. I'd feared that so much time apart, no matter how frequently we talked on the phone, would leave us strangers to each other.

That fear was put to rest when I found that I understood exactly what Creed meant. His statement was not meant to be harsh or insulting. It was merely an observation of how I'd changed. My own thoughts had been similar when I first saw him, the only difference was I had enough tact to keep those observations to myself.

Still chuckling, I finally felt comfortable enough to throw an arm over Creed's shoulder. "Ah, Creed. Blunt as ever. Yep, I've packed on a few pounds. There are so many places around the world with their own delicacies and unique tastes, and I refuse to be denied life pleasures for something as stupid as a waistline."

Just for emphasis, I patted my own stomach.

Never let anyone call me self-conscious.

"That sounds like good life advice."

The new voice had me turning around, where I found myself face to face with several people I didn't know. They stood a little distance away, giving Creed and I the illusion of privacy while still being able to hear everything we said. From

Creed's descriptions, I could already identify each of them. From the back of the little group, Trent and Ellis watched me with mild curiosity, while Brody and Magnus each gave me a hard stare. They were sizing me up, trying to determine if I was any threat to their friend.

A small, possessive part of me wanted to push back against that suspicion. I'd been Creed's friend long before they ever met him. If anyone should be protective of him, it should be me.

I shoved those thoughts to the farthest recess of my mind where hopefully even I would forget about them and kept the smile on my face.

"I wish my editor agreed with you. Pretty sure she thinks I'm a reckless idiot who's always getting into trouble."

Magnus crossed his arms over his chest and narrowed his blue eyes, but didn't' say a word.

Brody, on the other hand, kept a more

pleasant expression on his face, but he did raise an eyebrow at me in a subtle demand for answers.

"Is she right? Are you reckless?"

If they wanted to interrogate me, that was fine. It wasn't anything new. Whenever I showed up as a foreigner in a new place, the locals were always skeptical of me at first. However, half of my success as a travel writer came from my ability to earn local favor so they would eventually tell me the stories worth writing about.

We may still be in America, but on this particular patch of land, I was once again the foreign visitor.

Shoving my hands in my pockets, I let my shoulders slump a bit to soften my posture, but I still stood firm.

"I don't get paid to sit around and politely keep to myself. It's my job to get out there and experience what the world has to offer so other people can see it for themselves. Sometimes that means taking risks, but I try to make sure the danger is always calculated. I'm not stupid, I'm just not shy."

I'd taken my stand and made myself known. Now I waited for my verdict.

Before either Magnus or Brody could say anything, however, Creed grabbed my arm and started dragging me toward one of the houses.

"Come on, you dicks. Stop with the third degree. Kayden had a long drive out here and he's probably tired. He doesn't need you two bothering him."

I followed after Creed so he wouldn't have to drag me along, but out of the corner of my eye I noticed Magnus and Brody share a brief nod.

I'd been accepted.

Creed was a normally silent man, so his willingness to speak up for me probably did more than any argument I could have made.

CREED

Inside one of the houses, which I learned was Brody's house, dinner was just being set out on the table. An extra plate had already been set out for me, and I eagerly accepted the invitation. I'd skipped lunch while I was driving, not wanting to risk getting lost on unfamiliar roads, and sustained myself on snacks I could eat on the go. Chips and beef jerky were convenient, but not very filling, and the meal spread out before me looked amazing.

I was so hungry, I barely tasted the first few bites of it. They could have poisoned me, and I wouldn't have cared. The food was simple, but well made, and probably the closest thing to a "home cooked" meal I'd had in a long time.

Restaurants were all well and good, and I always tried as many as I could while traveling, but they lacked a certain warmth that could only be found in a meal made specifically for you.

Over the course of dinner, Trent and Ellis took the initiative to ask me about my work. I told them about some of the places I'd visited and was surprised to learn that they'd even read some of my articles. Eventually the topic of Covid came up, and the effect that the global lockdown a few years ago had on my work.

"It wasn't easy, of course," I said as I pushed my now empty plate away. "Not being able to go anywhere makes my job nearly impossible. But it wasn't as bad as I thought. During that time there was an uptick in interest for my older articles. Since everyone was stuck inside, I guess they instead lived vicariously through my writing."

"From what I saw online, a lot of your fans discovered you during Covid times," Ellis agreed. Despite his size, he was a soft-spoken man. I would expect someone like him to get overshadowed when surrounded by so many large personalities, but the others of this little group went out of their way to make sure he had just as many opportunities to speak as everyone else.

"You've been reading reviews from my fans? Uh oh. I hope they didn't have too many bad things to say about me."

Ellis quickly shook his head, his dark curls falling into his eyes. "Oh, no. Most people only said good things about your work. Although, there was one thing people kept mentioning that I didn't understand. What was the llama incident?"

Groaning, I hung my head in my hands. Of course that was coming back around to bite me in the ass.

"Okay, first, what you have to understand, the llama didn't look that dangerous."

***

I spent the night sleeping in the guest bedroom in Magnus's house. My original hopes of coming up with an excuse to room with Creed were dashed almost immediately when it was pointed out that, of the two houses on the property, each only had one guest room. Creed was already staying in the guestroom of Brody's house, so that left only one clear option for me.

It was a tragedy, but I consoled myself with the reminder that soon we'd be sharing a tent together. We'd have plenty of time to get... close... soon.

Although, that may not matter if he was already with someone. I still hadn't managed to determine the exact nature of his relationship with Magnus and Brody. It didn't seem like they were sexually involved, their body language wasn't quite right for that, but they were more protective of him than the average friends.

Of course, most average friends didn't

buy a property and build a home together, either.

By morning, I still didn't have any answers, and I looked forward to getting our camping trip started.

I'd been camping before, but that had been at a designated campground. This would be true wilderness camping. I could already picture the article I was going to write about it, and made sure to bring my laptop, camera, and plenty of supplies to document the whole trip.

Even if things didn't work out with Creed the way I hoped, I'd at least get a new experience out of it.

We were just finishing packing up the bags we were going to be carrying, when an unexpected visitor arrived at the property. I did a double take when I noticed a police car park next to my own rented vehicle. Despite all of my adventures, I'd only interacted with the police a few times. Yet, everyone else acted like the police suddenly showing up was a common occurrence. No one else was panicking, so I kept my own misgivings to myself.

"Deputy Hillard," Brody greeted the man who stepped out of the car. "What brings you here?"

The man, Deputy Hillard, eyed the large pit in the middle of the property. "Is it any surprise? Your little group here seems to get in trouble every time I turn my back." He paused for a moment when his gaze landed on me. "And you keep multiplying. Who are you?"

I opened my mouth, about to introduce myself, when Creed cut me off.

"He's a friend visiting from out of town. He's not involved in anything. What are you here for? Everything's been quiet with us, so there must be trouble on your end."

Deputy Hillard rubbed nervously at the back of his neck, giving the impression that he wasn't as old as he seemed at first.

"Not trouble, per say, but... well, I'm actually here for your help. It's about the items you found in that coffin. The locket, the key, and the journal."

Locket, key, and journal?

Creed had mentioned something about these items in relation to a dead body, but he made it sound like the case happened a while ago and was already closed.

Was there still an open investigation?

Creed, Magnus, and Brody all shared a look. It was clear some sort of silent communication happened, though they gave no indication of what they decided.

Brody stepped forward to invite Deputy Hillard onto the porch of his house. The large ginger man seemed to be the unofficial spokesperson of the group. I'd noticed that whenever an important conversation needed to happen, he was usually the one with the most words to say.

Knowing what I knew about Creed, that was probably for the best. My friend had a lot of talents, but words had always eluded him. Half the fights he got into in high school were mostly because he said something in the wrong way, or remained silent when he should have spoken.

There were only three chairs on the porch, so most of us were forced to remain standing. I chose to sit on the steps leading up to the porch. This position put me mostly out of sight, so I'd be overlooked, but still allowed me to clearly hear the conversation.

"The locket and the key have both been returned to police custody," Brody said, his wooden chair creaking as he slowly rocked back and forth. "The journal was stolen and still remains in the wind, but that is your responsibility. It has nothing to do with us."

Without even looking at Deputy

Hillard, I could tell the man was sweating where he sat. "The journal is what I wanted to talk to you about. Before it was stolen, we managed to take some pictures of its pages."

There was a rustling of paper, where I assumed the Deputy was showing Brody the photos in question.

Creed's almost silent footsteps stalked across the porch to get a better look for himself. "You've had these photos since the journal was first discovered. Why are you showing them to us now?"

Deputy Hillard hesitated for a moment. "Because we need your help. Look at the photos. The writing in the journal is complete gibberish. We assume it must be some sort of code, but we haven't been able to crack it."

I dared to peek around the railing porch railing, hoping to get a look at the photos for myself, but Brody was keeping them held close to his chest in a protective position, like he feared they would be snatched away at any moment.

"So, you're bringing this to us now in the hope that we can figure out the code for you," Brody mumbled half under his breath.

Off to the side, Magnus scoffed. "Typical. We've been the driving force behind every part of this case. At this point, I'm starting to wonder if there's a purpose to your police force even being involved. We shouldn't have to do your job for you."

Brody handed the photos over to Magnus, who immediately took them inside the house.

"We'll think about it," Brody said.

The Deputy started to argue, but Brody cut him off.

"Deputy Hillard. We've been threatened, kidnapped, hospitalized, had our property damaged, and gotten into multiple shootouts all because of this case. Surely, you understand why we're hesitant to involve ourselves any further."

In his seat, Deputy Hillard hung his head. "Yes, I... can understand that. But I do hope you'll help us so we can finally put this whole thing to rest."

"And as we said, we'll think about it," Magnus growled as he stepped back out onto the porch.

Brody nodded toward the deputy, and Magnus took that as his cue to escort the man to his car. Luckily, Deputy Hillard left without any further argument, and soon the black and white paint of his police cruiser disappeared into the trees.

"I assume you'll be helping them once again," Creed said when Magnus jogged up to join everyone else back on the porch.

Brody stood from the rocking chair, stretching his arms over his head until his spine audibly popped. "Of course. At this point, I doubt they could handle anything without our help. I just don't want them to get too comfortable making demands of us. Did you leave the photos in my office? Great. I'm going to go look at them. See what new challenge awaits us."

Everyone scattered in different directions after that. Ellis went with Brody, while Trent and Magnus went back to the other house.

That left me alone with Creed for the first time since I'd arrived. I would have loved to take advantage of the opportunity, but a heavier question weighed on my mind.

"Hey, Creed?"

He didn't jump, but I could tell from the widening of his eyes that he'd forgotten I was there.

"Kayden. Um... what's wrong?"

"What's wrong?" I repeated, insulted that he'd even ask that. "I don't know. You tell me. You mentioned that your friends found an old coffin on your property, but I thought that was already taken care of. Now it looks like that case is still being investigated. And Brody said you'd been kidnapped? Hospitalized? That sounds... that sounds really serious. So, tell me, what exactly is going on?"

CHAPTER THREE

Creed

IT WASN'T THE first time I'd escorted someone across hostile terrain. Many of my missions during my service had included getting a person of interest from point A to point B, preferably unharmed. Often these people had no survival instincts of their own, and they had been so reckless with their lives that I wondered if they legitimately wanted to die.

The situation with Kayden wasn't so

severe. The rough mountain terrain wasn't too hostile and shouldn't be a threat so long as we were careful. However, after only an hour after starting our trek, I quickly realized that he was ruled by his curiosity much more than his common sense.

"Don't go over there." I pulled Kayden back from where he'd been about to step off into the underbrush. There was no actual path, so we were following one of the natural trails formed by deer and other animals traveling through the area. I'd studied the area extensively from the moment we decided to purchase our property, so although I'd never been on this specific part of the mountain before, I knew we were going the right way.

Kayden, however, seemed determined to lead us astray.

He pouted at me, though he didn't stop me from physically pulling him back onto the trail.

"Why not? The way the sunlight filters through the trees over there would make for a great photo."

I'd expected Kayden to take extensive notes about our little camping trip. That was the whole reason for the journey, to give him something to write about.

What I hadn't expected was that he also insisted on photographing as much as possible. It shouldn't have come as a surprise. I'd read a few of his articles, and each was accompanied by plenty of pictures to show readers what he was describing, but I hadn't put the pieces together to realize what it would mean for our own trip.

Rather than try to explain to him why stepping off the trail was a bad idea, I decided to show him. Picking up a long stick lying on the ground nearby, I stuck it into the underbrush he'd been about to step through. The stick kept going, sinking down lower and lower so nearly the whole thing was below the leaves before it hit ground.

"Oh," Kayden gasped, pushing back some of the underbrush so he could see the hidden ravine for himself. "I didn't notice that at all. How'd you know that was there?"

"I've learned how to read the land," I said simply. "Come on. We need to keep going. At this rate we won't be reaching the camp site before nightfall."

Hitching his bag higher onto his back, Kayden hurried to follow after me as I started walking in the right direction again.

"Campsite?" he asked once he was walking next to me. "I thought this area was completely untamed."

I watched him out of the corner of my eye, noticing the way the large pack he was wearing weighed on him. Most people underestimated how heavy a properly stocked camping pack could be. I'd had a few escort missions fall apart simply because the person in question refused to carry their share of the load.

My gaze lingered on Kayden's body.

For all his reckless curiosity, he at least pulled his weight. I could tell he was struggling under the weight of his pack but he hadn't uttered a single word of complaint.

I'd been staring too long. Realizing what I was doing, I turned my gaze back to the path ahead of us. "It's not an official campground, but I've planned out safe areas for us to make camp. In wild areas like this, you can't just throw down a tent anywhere and assume it'll be safe."

"Uh huh," Kayden nodded absently as he pulled out a small journal and started taking notes. "And what makes a place safe for a tent? You said you haven't actually been out to this area before. How can you determine the best places to make camp ahead of time?"

Usually, I hated having my decisions questioned, especially by someone who clearly knew less than me. Yet, there was something about Kayden's tone that made his questions sound unobtrusive even as he grilled me for details. The genuine interest in my answers and his willingness to listen as much as talk made it easy to tell him what he wanted to know. As we continued our hike, I spent a surprisingly pleasant hour explaining about the various maps I'd consulted while planning out our trip, and how I'd used them to determine the best camping areas.

I'd answer these questions all day so long as he never asked me another question about the body that Magnus found or the rival cults of the area.

After Deputy Hillard's visit, I'd been forced to explain the basic situation to Kayden. Luckily, I'd been able to deflect most of his questions based on that fact that I hadn't actually been there. He'd been all geared up to interrogate Magnus and Brody about what happened to them, but I'd reminded him that we needed to leave soon. In this way, I'd managed to keep him from getting too involved, but I knew it wouldn't last forever. The man was too damn curious. Eventually, he'd be back on that train of questions, and I needed to figure out an answer to give him.

Around midday, when the sun was at its highest, we stopped for a break near a lake that we came across. I'd seen it on the map while I was planning out our route and thought it would make a good rest spot. I was right, but the squiggly blue shape on the map didn't convey anything about how beautiful it was. The water was crystal clear, reflecting the sky above us as if it were made of polished glass. Tall reeds waved in the breeze around the edge of the pond, creating a home for the horny frogs that sang to draw in a mate and the turtles that contentedly sunned themselves on whatever flat surface they could find.

This is what nature was supposed to look like. Untouched and left to thrive on its own without any interference from humans.

Unfortunately, land like this was becoming harder and harder to find.

Kayden stepped up next to me, holding a hand over his eyes to block the sun as he surveyed the scene.

Then he whistled low under his breath. "Damn. It's like something straight off a postcard. I've been to a lot of places around the world, but natural spots like this are always the best. A person could spend eternity here."

So could I, but we didn't have that kind of time.

"Half an hour," I told Kayden as I let my pack drop to the ground. "Then we need to keep going, or we won't get to the camping area in time."

He followed my example and took a seat on one of the large rocks near the edge of the lake.

Our timeframe actually wasn't' as bad as I made it sound. We were a little behind the pace I wanted to keep, but not as badly as I first feared. We'd get to our planned camping area later than I intended, but there would still be enough light for us to safely get everything set up.

I wasn't going to tell him that, though. Kayden would take it as an excuse to let his curiosity distract him even more.

The groan that Kayden let out when he sat down was loud enough to disturb some birds roosting in a tree nearby.

"Ugh. I don't know how you make this look so easy. I think my shoulders are about to fall off. It feels like I've been carrying another person on my shoulders all day."

"It's only been a few hours," I reminded him as I pulled out some trail rations from my pack. "And it's not the weight of a person. Your pack is only about forty pounds."

Kayden laughed, and his voice echoed out over the still surface of the lake.

"Oh. Only forty pounds. You say that like it's a small thing." When he realized I wasn't laughing, he gave me a dry look. "You know most people consider forty pounds to be a lot, right?"

No, I didn't. If anything, I'd consider it to be on the lighter side. Maybe forty had seemed like a lot of weight to me once, but interacting with him was quickly reminding me that I had no idea what "normal" was anymore.

I didn't answer him, and Kayden quickly lost interest. Instead, he occupied himself by taking photos of the lake. His camera clicked away, taking dozens of different shots, and soon, he forgot that he ever asked me a question.

While he was busy, I pulled out my phone and opened up the camera roll. Before leaving, I'd downloaded the pictures of the missing journal that Deputy Hillard brought us.

Based on what Brody and Magnus told me, the journal had probably belonged to Lisianthus Milford based on the etching of the flower on the book's metal clasp. I didn't know enough about flowers to identify the species from such a simple piece of artwork, so I'd have to take Magnus's word for it. The outside art of the journal didn't interest me anyway, only the words contained within.

The handwriting was rougher than expected. There were some attempts at adding flourish to the words here and there, but they were uneven and smeared in some spots. Whatever the owner of the journal had used to write with had obviously not been of good quality. Their pen left behind splotches of ink, and even poked right through the paper in some places.

It was also completely illegible, just as Deputy Hillard had said.

My first hope had been that the journal was simply written in a language that the Deputy didn't recognize, but the combinations of letters matched no language that I knew. It was written in the Latin alphabet, so the letters themselves were familiar, but other than that, the writing was complete gibberish.

It must be some sort of code.

Why else would someone go to so much effort to record a book full of nonsense?

If I had the whole journal, I'd probably be able to crack it eventually, but with only a few pages, I wasn't nearly as confident.

"What's that?" Kayden asked as he slid over next to me. "Talking to your friends back home."

I shoved the phone back in my pocket before the pictures could catch his attention.

"There's no cell service out here. I've got a satellite phone if we need to contact someone, but that's only for emergencies."

I handed over a portion of the trail rations, making sure he ate while he had the chance. It wouldn't be good for him to get so distracted he forgot to eat and then passed out later while we're walking.

Trail rations were meant to be nutritious, not necessarily taste good, but he ate them without complaint. He was halfway through his portion of the food when he suddenly spoke up again.

"But you want to talk to them."

It was such a non sequitur that I didn't understand what he meant at first.

"Your friends back home," he said, and I realized he was continuing the conversation from earlier as if there hadn't been any interruption. "I know that you only just retired from service and haven't been home very long. I'm sorry. I should have thought of that before dragging you out here with me. You must miss them."

I shrugged and took a sip of my water bottle to give my hands something to do. Whenever I was nervous or lost in thought, I tended to doodle on any nearby piece of paper. It was relaxing, and keeping my hands busy helped ease my mind, but out in the middle of the woods there was neither pen nor paper for me to use, so I had to make do.

"It's fine. If anything, I'm glad for the excuse to get away. Like I told you earlier, they've both... they've both got partners now. They've already started building their lives and I don't know how to fit into the new dynamic."

An awkward air hung around Kayden. I couldn't interpret it, and I didn't want to ask, so I let silence fall between us.

The birds that Kayden had scared off earlier returned, twittering away like they intended to chase him away just with the sound of their voices.

Kayden sighed.

"I was hoping I could figure out a more tactful way to ask you this, but I can't think of anything. So, I suppose I'll just have to come out and ask it. What... um, what is your relationship with Magnus and Brody?"

"What do you mean? We're friends."

"I know," Kayden quickly assured me, though he kept his gaze pointed out toward the lake rather than look me in the eye. "But, like, is it any more than that?"

I thought about it for a moment, and the answer was surprisingly obvious. "I suppose so. We've served together for years. They've saved my skin countless times, and I've saved them. At this point, we're more than friends. They're like my brothers."

I felt confident about this response, but Kayden only sighed again like he was disappointed.

"Yes, I'm sure serving together is a special kind of bond on its own, but I mean... Creed, come on. Normal friends don't build a home together. That implies something more intimate."

We were already past the half hour I'd allotted for our break, but any thought of continuing our journey disappeared from my mind as I stared at him blankly.

"Are you... are you asking me if I'm in some sort of threesome with Magnus and Brody."

Kayden grumbled under his breath. "Well, with their partners included it'd be more like a fivesome. Is that the right term? I don't know, but you get what I mean."

Unbidden, the image popped into my

head. The image of me with Brody and Magnus was already disturbing. To me, Magnus and Brody were like my brothers, and the thought of sleeping with them felt a lot like incest.

Adding in Trent and Ellis to the mix, however, took the disturbing thought and turned it comical. At first, I expected to be angry over Kayden's insinuation, but the image of all five of us trying to pile into the same bed was so ridiculous that I ended up laughing out loud.

"That's not— No, it's not like that. Brody, Magnus, and I are friends, but that's it. We decided to pool our money to buy a property together because the real estate market is fucked, and we could get a lot more together than we could apart. Besides, none of us had any family worth returning to, so we were free to build our home anywhere."

Kayden's voice was so small that I barely heard him when he said, "You could have come back to me."

It was said so quietly that I wasn't sure what he said at first, and by the time I processed his words, he was already standing up and reaching for his pack.

"Come on. You said we needed to reach the campsite before nightfall, right? We should get going."

He started walking in the wrong direction, and I had to quickly grab my own pack and run after him to keep him from getting lost. Although I knew that we should discuss Kayden's last remark, it was clear he wanted to move on and forget he'd said anything. I had never been very good with conversation, even under the best circumstances. So, I chose the coward's way out and let the matter drop. Our conversation eventually turned toward our plans once we made camp—where I had to explain exactly what that would entail—and it was as if Kayden's questions by the lake never happened.

I was left with a mix of guilt and relief. Guilt that I had clearly upset my friend somehow, and relief that I didn't have to navigate such a difficult conversation.

Facing down a swarm of armed combatants, or flying a rescue chopper through enemy airspace, no problem. I could charge forward without hesitation. Yet an emotional conversation had me running scared with my tail between my legs.

I would have slapped myself for my cowardice if I didn't think it would make me look insane.

On a positive note, we made better progress in the second half of the day and managed to reach the planned campsite with half an hour of sunlight left.

The trees were very dense in this part of the forest. It would give us good shelter from the wind and keep the rain off us if the weather turned bad. There was a small area near the base of a stony cliff with just enough space for us to pitch a tent and make a fire.

"Are you sure you can handle the tent?" I asked Kayden as I started setting out stones to form a ring around the campfire to keep it contained.

"Yeah, I'll be fine," he assured me. His voice was confident, but in the dim light of dusk I was just able to see uncertainty flash though his eyes.

I chose not to point it out and focused on collecting firewood. With so many trees nearby, I didn't need to go far, but I took my time to give Kayden an opportunity to work on the tent without feeling like he was being watched.

It reminded me of my first expedition in boot camp. One of our trainers took a bunch of new recruits out into the woods to practice basic survival skills. I'd grown up in a major city and had rarely ever even seen a tree that wasn't growing out of a hole in the concrete. I'd never built a fire or pitched a tent. Suddenly dropped in the middle of the forest, I had no idea what I was doing, and as it turned out, all the other new recruits had been avid campers.

I'd felt like a total idiot, struggling to set up my tent while everyone else had been done within minutes. They pretended not to watch me, but I could feel their stares on my back.

Their silent judgment had burned me worse than if I'd just stuck my hand straight in the fire. After that, I'd signed up for every survival class that I could until I became the leading expert, but the sting of that first failure never went away.

I never wanted to make Kayden feel that way, so I hung around in the woods, slowly collecting firewood until enough time had passed for him to flip through the tent's directions and figure out the basics for himself.

When I finally returned, the tent still

wasn't up, but he'd figured out how to put the support poles together, which was the first step.

"Need any help?" I offered as I set my pile of firewood down.

He waved me off over his shoulder. "No, no. I've got this. It's simple."

"Okay. I'll leave you to it, but feel free to ask for help if you need it."

"I'm fine," he insisted again, but at that exact moment one of the support poles slipped out of his grip and snapped him on the hand. He yelped, then bit his lip to silence himself as he shook out his hand.

I swallowed my laughter and turned back to my fire pit.

Nightfall descended on the mountain just as I finished getting the fire set up. It was summer, so the nights didn't get too cold, but the warmth was still comforting. The soft orange light of the fire fended off the gloom of the forest and created an almost homey atmosphere around us.

"How's it coming?" I asked when I turned back to Kayden. He'd done surprisingly well with the tent. It wasn't perfect, a little lopsided and the ground anchors weren't hammered in far enough, but it was better than my first attempt had been.

Just as I opened my mouth to compliment him, a pair of glowing eyes caught my attention.

On a ledge of the cliff sticking out just above the spot where Kayden was setting up the tent, a mountain lion was crouched and ready to pounce. Its sandy fur blended into the stone, making it invisible in the shadows. If not for the glint of firelight reflecting off its eyes, I never would have seen it.

My body acted on instinct. I dove and tackled Kayden out of the way just as the mountain lion pounced. The creature landed right where he'd been kneeling, its claws digging deep grooves into the dirt.

Kayden gasped when he hit the ground, trapped under my weight. He shoved at my shoulder, demanding to know what I was doing, but froze when he heard the large cat growl.

"What is that?" He tried to look around my shoulder, but I shoved him farther back. "Oh my God."

"Kayden, get out of the way," I snapped at him. There was no time to check that he followed my directions. The mountain lion was furious after missing its target and turned on us with even more determination.

Getting my feet under me, I pulled the knife from my belt and met the creature head on.

There must be something wrong with it. Mountain lions were fierce creatures, but they didn't usually go after full-grown adult humans for no reason. Maybe in the middle of winter, if the creature was starving, I could understand. However, it was summer, and there had to be plenty of much easier prey for it to go after.

A quick glance confirmed that the mountain lion was male, so it couldn't be a mother defending cubs.

It must be sick and acting irrationally. Unfortunately, that would only make the fight harder. An irrational opponent couldn't be predicted.

The cat swiped at me, its claws extended, but didn't press the attack farther. It was only testing my strength.

I couldn't let it perceive me as weak.

Standing to my full height and extending my arms out from my body, I made myself look as big as possible. The knife remained clutched in my hand, and I shifted my weight to the balls of my feet, ready to react at a moment's notice.

The cat swiped again, a little closer now. I blocked its paw with my knife, letting it feel the sharpness of the blade.

It's claws barely touched the steel, but the force of the blow was enough to send a numb vibration up my arm. It was only about three feet tall, but solid muscle. Taking it down would not be easy.

I could shoot it if necessary. There was a gun in my pack, which I might be able to grab if I hurried, but I didn't want to kill it if I didn't have to. This wild animal was no enemy combatant. It was simply a creature fighting for its life. There would be no honor in killing it.

The flickering firelight made the mountain lion's expression look like something straight out of a nightmare as it snarled at me. Its teeth were sharp and long, and even more intimidating than my knife.

Its back legs hunched. It was about to lunge again.

Before it could move, I charged forward instead. The cat startled, not expecting the sudden attack. Its hesitation gave me just enough time to drag my knife across the side of its flank. The cut was deep, and blood immediately stained its tawny fur. I hoped the injury wouldn't be fatal, but I couldn't afford to hold back anymore.

I'd avoided a killing blow. That would have to be enough.

Still facing the cat, I stepped back while keeping myself between it and Kayden, waiting to see what would happen.

The pain left by my knife seemed to be enough to temporarily shock the creature out of whatever insanity had taken hold of it. Shaking its head, the mountain lion whined and backed off, slowly slipping out of the circle of light created by our fire.

I stayed where I was, bloodied knife still held tight in my hand, as I tracked the faint shadow of the creature in the dark. It hung around for a little longer, just out of sight. It seemed to be looking for a better angle of attack. After several tense minutes, it eventually gave up and disappeared back into the trees. I continued to stay on alert for a little longer, but when it was clear that the creature wasn't coming back, I finally relaxed.

I knelt down and wiped my blade on the grass to get rid of the blood. I would have to clean it properly later, but many people found blood to be a frightening sight, and I didn't want to stress Kayden out anymore.

"Sorry about that," I said as I shoved my knife back in its sheath. "Are you all right?"

He was still lying in the dirt where I'd shoved him. It was a miracle I hadn't stepped on him during the fight. He seemed completely frozen, staring up at me with an astonished expression.

He didn't seem to have heard me at all.

He wasn't even blinking, and even when I repeated myself, he still didn't respond.

I resorted to shouting his name, the same way my drill sergeant used to scold me. This finally got a reaction. Kayden jumped to his feet, moving too quickly and tripping over himself. I caught him before he fell, pulling him closer to help support him.

"It's okay," I tried to soothe him. I'd seen people suffer from shellshock after their first run-in with violence, and I was afraid that's what I was witnessing now. "The creature probably won't come back now that it's been scared off. We should be safe now, and if it does come back, I promise I'll protect you."

He slid his hands up and gripped my shoulders. At first, I thought he was just trying to steady himself, but then he pulled me forward and kissed me.

I didn't even realize it was a kiss at first. I'd never actually kissed another man before, and the few kisses I'd exchanged with women had been brief, hesitant exchanges done mostly out of obligation. This was heated and intense. His lips parted and his tongue forced its way into my mouth like he intended to devour me.

I was too stunned to move and let him do whatever he wanted.

The kiss lasted for a few moments, but then Kayden suddenly tensed up and pushed me away. Clamping both hands over his own mouth, he backed away until he was well out of arms reaching. As he started at me, his eyes were filled with more fear than he'd even shown for the mountain lion.

I hated that expression.

"I'm sorry," he gasped out from between his fingers, still holding his hands over his mouth. "I didn't mean to. I've just... I've never actually seen you in action before. I knew you were a soldier, but I didn't expect... I mean, you were just so hot I couldn't help it."

He backed away even farther, all the way to the edge of the firelight so he was half concealed in shadow.

Lowering his hands from his mouth, he nervously twisted at the hem of his own shirt like a child waiting to be punished.

"I'm so sorry. Please tell me I haven't just ruined everything."

CHAPTER FOUR

Kayden

PANIC FILLED MY head with an endless string of curses.

How could I have jumped Creed like that?

The man had just barely admitted to being gay, and clearly still wasn't very comfortable with the idea. Now I'd probably ruined whatever chance I had with him.

Hell, I'd probably ruined our friendship as well.

I waited for him to yell at me, or maybe even turn around and leave me on this mountain to find my own way home.

Instead, he remained silent. His face didn't even twitch with the slightest hint of emotion. Creed had always been a stoic person, but even for him this was extreme.

It seemed I'd broken him.

I didn't know what to do, so I did what I always did when I was uncertain.

I kept running my mouth.

"You're upset. I get it. I would be, too, if someone kissed me without permission. I don't have any excuse, but I just... I just couldn't help it." I started pacing, covering the diameter of our little camp in just a few steps before turning around and going the other direction. "I never should have even come on this trip. It was stupid, but when I realized you were gay, I thought maybe I had a chance, and I just had to come see you. My publisher was planning on sending me to the Himalayas, but I begged them to let me do a domestic piece. I'm sorry. I shouldn't have lied to you."

My pacing was brought to an abrupt halt when Creed grabbed my arm.

"Stop talking."

Before I could utter another word, he dragged me over to the tent and shoved me inside. I tripped and landed on the sleeping bags, which I'd thankfully, already set up. Rolling onto my back, the demand for an explanation was already on the tip of my tongue, when Creed pinned me down to the ground and kissed me.

We were roughly the same size, but Creed was built with a lot more muscle after so many years of training. I could barely move under him, and I had no hope of pushing him off.

Not that I wanted to. Once I realized what was happening, I wrapped my arms around him and pulled him even closer.

For all of Creed's confidence, he was surprisingly uncoordinated when it came to kissing. The man seemed to have no idea what to do with his tongue after shoving it in my mouth, and his lips didn't move at all.

It was, truthfully speaking, a bad kiss.

That was all right. I was an eager instructor.

Cupping his head between my hands, I tilted him until we were at a better angle for our mouths to align. Gentle coaxing showed him how to coordinate his lips and tongue, and soon enough, the kiss turned from awkward to pleasant.

We eventually had to part for air, but I didn't let him get far and continued to press small kisses to the corner of his mouth.

"This is great, Creed, but I need you to use your words," I said between kisses. "Say that you want to sleep with me."

One of his hands plucked at my shirt, tugging at it like it was a stress toy.

"I think I do."

I pulled back from the kiss enough to look him in the eye.

"You think?"

An unfairly charming blush spread across his cheeks, visible even in the low light.

"I don't know. I've never done this before. But, yes, I think I do."

He tried to kiss me again, but I pressed a hand against his chest and pushed him back enough so I could sit up.

"Wait. You've never done this before? Like, never slept with a man? Then how do you know for sure that you're gay?"

Sitting there in the tent that was barely big enough for the two of us, with his head brushing against the top of the canvas, he gave me the flattest look I'd ever seen.

"The same way that I don't need to

fuck a kid to know that I'm not a pedophile."

The shock of his crude words made me choke on my own spit. I coughed violently for several moments until I could breathe again.

"Okay, first of all, ew." Tears gathered in my eyes for the force of my coughing, and I knocked myself in the chest a few times to get my lungs working again. "But, point taken, I guess. So, you're certain about this, right? I don't want to suddenly regret things in the morning."

To his credit, he did legitimately think about it for a moment.

"Yes, I'm sure," he eventually said. "I wouldn't be comfortable sleeping with a stranger, and the only other people I'm close enough with to even consider are Magnus and Brody, and they're obviously not an option."

I would have been insulted by his insinuation that I was simply the only option, except I knew Creed. The man did not settle for anything. He'd give something up entirely before he settled for second best. I'd once watched the man turn down a free sundae simply because they didn't have the exact flavor he wanted.

Now, ice cream wasn't nearly as important as sex and relationships, but the principle was the same. If Creed agreed to sleep with me, it was only because he'd decided that I was exactly what he wanted.

"All right," I practically cheered, happy to have gotten that cleared up. "You're lucky that I brought some stuff. We'll have to get it out of my bag. I thought I was being overly optimistic, but now it's paying off."

Creed just looked at me, confused. "What stuff?"

At first, I thought he was joking, but his expression was a hundred percent serious.

I gaped at him. "You know, like, condoms and stuff. How do you not..." I trailed off as a thought occurred to me. "Creed? You said you've never slept with a man, but I assumed that meant you'd at least slept with women. You have had sex before, right?"

The idea of a man, especially someone as appealing as Creed, making it all the way to his forties without ever having sex seemed preposterous. That was the kind of thing that only happened in romantic comedies.

Rather than answer me immediately, he grabbed my bag from where we'd stored it under a tarp outside the tent.

"That depends on your definition," he muttered as he started unzipping various pockets. It was clear he didn't know what he was looking for, but just needed something to do with his hands.

Reaching into the right pocket, I pulled

out a small, nondescript black bag that I hadn't expected to actually use when I packed it. "Depends on the definition? What does that mean?"

"It means, it depends on how far you think something has to go for it to be considered sex."

I was tempted to demand further explanation, but in the end, I decided I didn't want to know. Hearing the details of Creed's past exploits would just end up making me jealous.

I was reminded of when I was a teenager, deciding to have sex for the first time. It was right after Creed had left for the military, at the ripe age of eighteen, and I was determined to finally get over my longstanding crush on him. I'd thought sex would fix it, and hooked up with the first willing person I could find. It hadn't worked, but my partner had been surprisingly supportive and walked me through my first time. At the time, I would have considered dating that young man if he was interested in anything other than a one-night stand.

Now, years later, I didn't even remember the name of my first partner, but I did remember the way he explained everything he was doing before he did it. That explanation helped keep me calm in an overwhelming situation, and I hoped it would help Creed now.

Step one was to get our clothes off, which I thought would be the easy part, but even that ended up being more complicated than it needed to be when Creed insisted on folding all his clothes first. I would have been annoyed by the delay if I didn't find it so cute.

It was a shame the tent was so dark. Even in the dim light of the campfire, I could tell that Creed had a good body. Muscular in all the right places, with a dark thatch of chest hair that would be fun to run my fingers through, but he was also soft enough around the middle to be comfortable.

And his thighs....

I could have written an entire article about his thighs, though my fans probably wouldn't want to read it. They were thick as barrels and corded with muscles that flexed every time he moved. I couldn't resist reaching out giving one a squeeze to feel the hard flesh under my hand.

I wondered if I could get off just from fucking his thighs. If tonight went well, I'd have to suggest it next time.

When we were both finally undressed, the next step was to apply the condom. I'd already decided to bottom this time since that would be easier for Creed, but I hadn't thought ahead enough to realize that meant I'd be putting the condom on him. I nearly came on the spot when I took his cock in hand for the first time.

Damn, the man was well built here,

too. It was a good thing I had plenty of experience in both positions, or this would have been a rough ride.

I nearly laughed aloud when I saw the look of concentration on Creed's face as I explained exactly how to apply the condom. It was like he was studying for a test, and he was determined to get a passing grade. The temptation to mess with him was too strong. Once I had the condom on, I stroked him a few times and watched him gasp at the pleasure that suddenly hit him.

"You don't have to be so serious," I said, still trying hold back my laugher. Then, right as he was about to respond, I twisted my hand over the head of his cock in a way that I knew would feel especially good.

"I don't— Ah!" He squirmed in place and squeezed his eyes shut tight to try and control himself. "I don't want to make any mistakes."

"Creed..." I sighed and shook my head, even as I continued to stroke him. "This isn't a test. There's no way to 'fail'. As long as you don't, like, accidentally stick it up my nose or something, then you'll be fine."

The look of horror that washed over his face was so comical I had to bite my lip to keep from laughing.

"Can that happen?"

He was completely serious, and I could see the wheels turning in his head as he tried to picture it.

"No," I managed to gasp out, my shoulders shaking with the effort of holding back my laughter. "I was just exaggerating to make a point. It'll be fine."

It was a testament to Creed's virility that, despite his brief moment of fear, his erection never flagged. If anything, he was harder than ever. It was more than I could've managed. Even the slightest negative emotion usually killed my libido immediately.

Or maybe he was just that horny. The man was still basically a virgin at forty-four. That had to come with a lot of pent-up sexual frustration.

With the condom in place, the last step was to prepare myself. I was an expert at this.

How many nights had I lied awake in bed, fingering myself to completion while imagining it was Creed between my legs?

Too many. Certainly, more than I was willing to admit.

However, before this it had always just been imaginative. Over the years, Creed had become a fantasy that I fell back on for comfort whenever I was lonely, or my love life wasn't going well. In some ways, it was no different than a child with an imaginary friend.

Now, Creed was right in front of me, doing things I'd only ever dreamed of. As I lay back on the sleeping bags and reached down between my legs to prepare myself, I was struck with a sudden flair of anxiety.

What if reality didn't live up to my imagination?

Would I be disappointed?

And if I was, would Creed notice?

Would my expectations ruin everything before we even started?

I slipped my fingers inside myself, lubricant easing their way, but I barely noticed. I was too caught up in my own head.

The unexpected touch of a hand wrapping around my cock shocked me back to reality.

Creed knelt between my legs, his expression uncertain, as he stroked me the same way that I'd pleasured him earlier.

"You seemed like you were struggling," he said without fully looking at me. "Is getting yourself ready that difficult?"

No, I was just so caught up in my own

worries that I was killing my own arousal. But I wasn't going to tell him that.

Instead, I put on my best flirtatious expression and canted my hips to push myself more firmly against his hand.

"Just stretching myself a little more than usual. You're bigger than any previous partner. I gotta make sure I'll be able to take you."

He narrowed his eyes for a moment, and I wondered if he was jealous over the mention of previous partners.

I hoped so.

That would mean he cared about me as more than just a sexual partner.

Well, even if all he wanted from me was sex, I'd happily give it to him. Hell, I probably wouldn't even mind if he wanted to sleep with other people as well, so long as I was in the rotation.

Was that healthy?

No.

Did I care?

Also no.

Eventually, I determined myself ready—or as ready as I was going to get—and removed my fingers from my hole. I then spread my legs farther and encouraged him to come closer.

"So, that's it?" he said as he looked down at me. "I just…"

"Put it in?" I finished for him. "Well, I hope you'll have a little more finesse than that. Here. I'll help you."

Taking his cock in hand again, I guided him to my pucker and encouraged him to push inside. It was a bit awkward at first. He didn't know how much force to use, and his first couple of thrusts weren't very effective. However, eventually, he got the hang of it, and he was soon sliding inside of me in one smooth motion.

I groaned and threw my head back. The man felt even bigger than I thought. Almost on the verge of too much. Luckily,

I didn't mind a little pain with my pleasure and kept myself relaxed. I could feel every inch of him as he pressed deeper and deeper until I could barely breathe. If I didn't know better, I would have thought Creed had found a way to bury himself directly into my lungs, I felt so full.

Once he was all the way inside, Creed froze. My eyes were still squeezed shut, so I couldn't see his expression, but I could feel his uncertainty.

"Now what should I do?"

Still keeping myself relaxed, I settled in against the padding of the sleeping bag.

"Just move in whatever way feels good. We can experiment and see what you like best."

He tentatively pulled out, only daring to move an inch or two before pushing back in. Even that small thrust made him gasp and pull back a little more the second time.

It was a strange sensation for me. Pleasant, but not stimulating enough for me to get off from it. It didn't matter. This time was for Creed. The man needed an opportunity to figure out what he liked. Then we could chase our pleasure together.

He quickly gained confidence, and soon, he was pulling almost all the way before thrusting back in with enough force to jolt my whole body.

I watched him as if in a trance. He followed my instructions, changing the angle of his hips with each thrust to find what felt best. He sped up and slowed down, experimenting with so many new sensations.

Even if someone gave me a million-dollar book deal, I couldn't have properly described what I felt in that moment. My body was no longer my own. It was a tool for Creed to use as he wished.

It was a strange kind of pleasure, the

likes of which I'd never known before. Physically, I felt good as he moved inside me, managing to hit several of my most sensitive spots despite his inexperience. But what I really enjoyed was the sense of power it gave me, watching him use my body. I was the thing giving him pleasure in that moment, and I could take it away if I wanted. But I wouldn't. I never would. I wanted to give him everything, and I loved watching him indulge in me.

I'd never felt powerful when I submitted to someone before. It had always been pleasant, but it also felt like an obligation. Like my partner and I had to work to make sure everything was equally pleasant for both of us.

Now, even if I didn't finish, I wouldn't care. I was giddy to the point of euphoria as I let Creed use me.

I could tell he was near his end when his expression changed. The man didn't make much sound other than the occasional soft grunt, but the higher his pleasure grew, the more his whole body tensed up. Just as he was reaching his limit, I cupped his face and pulled him down into a kiss.

He groaned against my mouth as he came. His hips jerked sporadically against me, rubbing our whole bodies together. I didn't expect to find my own pleasure, but we were pressed so closely together than my cock was trapped between both of our stomachs. The stimulation from all sides sent a thrilling jolt up my spine, and I found myself tipping over the edge of my own orgasm as well.

I held him tight, arms and legs both locked around him as we trembled together. My mouth never left him for more than a moment, determined to share every breath he took.

The night air was cool, but the space within our tent blazed with the heat emanating off both of our bodies. We were both dripping with sweat, and one of my legs slipped from around his hips. My foot struck against one of the tent poles and I felt something shift.

Then the whole canvas structure collapsed around us.

We stared at each other in shock as we realized what had happened. The ceiling of the tent was now draped over Creed's head like a veil, cutting us both from the light of the campfire so we were barely able to see each other.

Letting his forehead rest against mine, Creed started laughing.

I joined him a moment later.

"I guess my tent building skills aren't as good as I thought."

Very softly, Creed pressed a kiss to my forehead. "At least it held out until we finished."

Extracting ourselves from the fallen tent was an adventure all on its own. It took us several minutes to find the opening and crawl out of the mess of canvas and support poles.

Then, after cleaning ourselves up and putting on fresh clothes, we set about fixing the tent up properly this time. I let Creed take the lead, following his instructions on how to properly anchor the support poles and string the canvas so it wouldn't collapse on us a second time.

According to Creed's fancy tactical watch—which was basically a digital watch that had been designed to withstand the elements better than an ordinary watch—it was past eleven at night when we finally settled down to sleep.

There wasn't much space inside the tent, so I was already pressed up against Creed's side, but I kept my hands to myself at first. Just because Creed was interested in sex didn't mean he'd want to cuddle afterward.

However, when he didn't object to my close proximity, I gave in to my curiosity and let my hands wander over his chest. I'd noticed before that he had several tattoos, but there hadn't been a good chance to study them closely until now.

Most of them were on his upper body, though I knew there were a few on his legs as well. Each looked to have been made by a different artist. Some were hyper realistic, while some had a more classic tattoo style. Some were just a few words, while others showed a scene.

One of the tattoos on his chest caught my attention. At first, I thought it was a cross, but upon closer inspection I realized it was actually helicopter blades viewed from above.

"I got that one done right after the rescue I made as a chopper pilot," Creed answered my unspoken question.

I slowly traced the outline of each blade. "Is that what you mostly did?

Rescuing people?"

"Sometimes," he said, though there was a wistful air to his tone that told me there was a lot more to the story. "One way or another, it was often my job to get people through hostile territory."

"Will you tell me about it some day?"

He paused for a moment before pulling my hand away from his tattoo to tuck it between us instead. "Maybe. Now, go to sleep. We've got a busy day tomorrow."

Even after he closed his own eyes, he continued to hold onto my hand. I took that as permission to cuddle up next to him and draped one of my legs across his hips to pull him as close as possible.

I was still ecstatic over everything we'd done together, and the last edges of adrenaline hadn't fully left my system. I could feel my veins buzzing under my skin.

Yet, I was also exhausted, and when I closed my eyes, I fell asleep almost instantly.

***

From the first moment I woke up the next morning, I felt like I was a teenager again. I couldn't keep my eyes off Creed. From preparing our breakfast over the campfire, to packing up the tent and other supplies, my gaze was drawn to him every time he moved.

It was just like high school all over again.

Just over an hour after sunrise, we were packed up and ready to continue our hike. My bag was no different than before, but I swore it felt ten pounds lighter.

"Creed?" I asked after we'd been walking for a few minutes. "Did you do something to my pack?"

His silence was answer enough.

"You did! You put more of the supplies in your own bag. Why? I can carry my own weight on this trip."

He mumbled something I couldn't hear then started walking faster.

"What was that? Hey, don't walk away from me. Explain yourself."

He slowed down so I could catch up, but still kept his eyes pointed forward.

"You're limping."

"What?"

I stopped frozen in the middle of the trail, wondering if Creed was hallucinating.

Then the ache in my back reminded me of our activities of last night, and I realized what he meant.

"Creed," his name dripped from my lips, half spoken word and half laughter. "It's not that bad. Okay, yes, there's a slight hitch in my step. What can I say? You're a big boy, and you really worked me over last night. But it's nothing I'm not used to. I'll be fine. You don't need to carry my supplies for me."

I tried to unclip one of the extra bags

that was strapped to his main pack so I could add it to my own, but he danced out of my reach.

"I caused your discomfort," he insisted. "So, I'll shoulder the responsibility."

"That doesn't have to be so literal." I tried to grab the bag again, but he easily maneuvered away from me. "Creed, come on. Stop being so stubborn."

"Stop being so reckless with your own health."

He turned his back on me, intending to walk away now that he'd made the final decision.

I wasn't going to be thwarted so easily.

If I made another grab for the bag right away, he was bound to notice. So, I waited. After another hour of hiking, I sidled up next to him, letting my hand trail up his arm in a teasing manner. He gave me a suspicious glance, but didn't try to stop me, so I went in for the kill. Leaning closer, I pressed a quick kiss to the side of his neck.

It worked. A shiver traveled up Creed's spine, which he tried to hide, but I could still see it from such closer proximity.

I placed another kiss on his neck, then behind his ear, then traveled down his jaw until I eventually reached his mouth. Once I had him locked into a proper kiss, I pushed him backward until I had him pressed up against a tree.

It was a make-out session worthy of any teenage romance. I slotted my leg between his, letting my thigh rub against his erection through his pants, just to make sure he was thoroughly distracted.

Then I reached for the bag again.

My hand never made it to its destination. The tips of my fingers just barely managed to brush cloth when my wrist was suddenly surrounded with an iron grip. Creed held my hand tight, keeping me from reaching my goal.

"You're sneakier than I remember,

Kay."

There was a dark, husky edge to his voice that I'd never heard before. Not even when he'd been fucking me last night. The promises he made, just from the sound of that voice, left me breathless.

Before I realized what was happening, he flipped me around, so I was the one pressed against the tree. My hands were pinned above my head, and his hips pressed tight against mine, trapping me in place.

"I'm going to have to keep my guard up around you," he said. The breath of his words ghosted against my lips, right before he kissed me.

Rough bark dug into my scalp as I angled my head to deepen the kiss. I was fully prepared to let him take me right then and there, but after only a few tantalizing moments, he pulled away and left me gasping.

"Later," he said, sounding too

composed for my liking. "We need to keep going now."

"You…" I panted for breath, struggling to regain my wits after he'd sucked them right out of my head. "You bastard. You're just a damn tease, that's what you are."

Creed laughed, but he didn't stop or turn around. There would be no arguing with him. The man had gotten his way, and he knew it.

I started to follow him, when a sharp prick in my neck made me stop. Assuming it was a bug, I slapped at the spot, but that only made the pain worse. There was something hard imbedded in my neck.

Pulling it out, I held the strange object up in front of my eyes.

It looked like a dart.

I should have recognized what it was immediately, but I'd never seen such a thing outside of an action movie.

It was a tranquilizer dart.

I started to call for Creed, but his name wasn't even halfway out of my mouth when the dart's effects hit. The world spun around me for a moment. Then, all at once, like being pulled under by strong ocean wave, I tumbled into oblivion.

***

Drugged unconsciousness wasn't the same as properly sleeping. There was no sense of falling asleep or waking up. One moment I was awake, then everything went black.

Then, what felt like only a moment later, I was awake again.

My mouth felt weird, like it was stuffed with cotton. It reminded me of the one time I'd gotten drunk enough to black out. I'd woken up with such a disgusting taste in my mouth—not to mention the pounding headache—that I swore to never drink again.

That promise hadn't lasted, but I never again pushed my alcohol tolerance to the point of blacking out.

This almost felt the same, but there was one distinct difference. I wasn't imaging the feeling of cotton filling my mouth.

It was real.

My eyes shot open. I was surrounded by darkness, so I couldn't tell where I was, but I was gagged by a strip of cloth tied around my head.

The metal floor under me was painfully cold. I tried to sit up but was immediately halted. My hands were tied behind my back and attached to something behind me.

That was when everything caught up to me and I realized what had happened.

I'd been kidnapped.

I started to hyperventilate, breathing rapidly through my nose since my mouth was blocked.

Why would anyone kidnap me?

I'd never made any enemies. I'd never even got into a fight with anyone.

And how had they kidnapped me?

Last I remembered, I'd been out in the middle of the forest, halfway up a mountain with Creed.

Creed!

Had he been captured too, or was he wandering around that mountain wondering where I'd gone?

While I was lost in my panic, my eyes slowly adjusted to the dark until I could finally make out the shape of my surroundings. It was a small room, only a few feet wide, and there was something large lying right next to me.

Something distinctly human-shaped.

My legs weren't bound, so I tapped the shape with my foot. It was soft, like a human would be, but I couldn't see well enough to tell if it was Creed or not.

The floor beneath us jostled. I fell back

and my head hit the wall. Stars danced in front of my eyes, and I groaned in pain as I blinked rapidly to clear my vision.

When I could see again, I noticed that the other person had shifted slightly. I could see part of their arm, revealing a familiar tattoo.

The other person was Creed after all.

I couldn't decide if that was a good thing or a bad thing. Part of me was relieved that he was here, but another part of me wished he was far away.

He seemed to still be unconscious. I couldn't see if he was breathing or not, but I refused to believe anything else. He had to just be unconscious.

The floor moved again, and I struggled to remain sitting upright.

Wait, why was the floor moving?

Now that it had caught my attention, I realized that all the walls and floor around us were constantly moving slightly. Most of the time it was too faint to notice, but every now and then everything would suddenly jump.

We weren't in a room. We were in the back of a vehicle.

Squinting at one of the walls, I could just see the outline of a pair of doors. It looked like we were in the back of a large van.

I stretched out one of my legs toward the door, but I was at least two feet short of reaching them. They were probably locked, but even if I could open them it wouldn't matter. My hands were chained to the wall. I wasn't going anywhere.

There was nothing I could do as the van continued to carry us off.

Wherever we were headed, it couldn't be anywhere good.

CHAPTER FIVE

Creed

THE NIGHT WAS so brilliant above us. It was the kind of sky only scene in movies. A full moon, the Milky Way in full view, and even the occasional shooting star just for ambiance. Nights like these reminded me of why I felt more comfortable out in nature than cooped up in civilization. Humans were complicated, but the wild elements were simple and easy to understand.

Kayden and I had pitched our tent

properly this time, without any mountain lions to distract us. We'd made good progress during the day's hike, so there was plenty of extra time to enjoy the sunset and relax while stargazing.

Well, I would have been relaxing, but the way Kayden lay pressed up against me, trailing kisses up and down my throat was only making me more excited.

He'd taken most of the lead last night, instructing me on what to do. Maybe this time I could take care of him instead.

"Let's close the tent," I said when I couldn't take his teasing anymore. "We don't need bugs snacking on us while we're busy."

He mumbled something against my throat, but I couldn't understand him.

"What?" I pulled him away from me so I could hear him.

He gave me a warm, familiar smile. The kind that had always comforted me, even when we were kids. I'd had a hard

time making friends when I was young—
and even as an adult—but with Kayden it
had always been easy.

Looking at me with eyes like crescent
moons, he repeated himself.

I furrowed my brow. I still couldn't
hear him. His mouth moved, but his voice
was muffled as if someone were pressing
a pillow over his face.

Something wasn't right. The longer I
looked at his face, the more it seemed off.
There weren't as many lines around his
eyes as there should be, making him
seem younger than he actually was, like a
combination of his current self and the
young man that I'd known before joining
the service. The exact color of his hair
shifted between different shades of brown.

He didn't look like himself, but rather
like an image created by an artist from
memory.

A moment of clarity struck me, and I
realized I was dreaming. I reached for the

tent flap, intending to flee, but the moment I touched the canvas, the material changed right under my hand. Instead of canvas, I was now gripping onto a stone wall, gritty and damp like a basement that hadn't been cleaned in decades.

Something struck me hard across the face, knocking me to the floor.

This couldn't be a dream.

It felt too real.

With my head still spinning from the blow, I pushed myself off the floor. The taste of dust and copper coated my tongue. I was grinning, and I could feel my own blood staining my teeth. I probably looked deranged.

Good.

Whoever had dared to strike me should be afraid.

I was ready to fight back, to make my enemy regret ever challenging me, but when I looked up, I found myself facing a nightmare.

"No," I gasped as I took in the new scene around me. "No, this can't be."

I'd seen this room before. It had been my prison once.

No, it was my prison *right now.*

Several other people were chained to the walls, either unconscious or dead, I couldn't tell.

I recognized them. I'd known these faces for years. Magnus and Brody were there, battered and bloody. Even Kayden hung on the wall. He was so still he didn't seem to be breathing.

Clutching my head, I started to hyperventilate.

No, this wasn't right. There was no reason for them to be here, together.

In this room.

When I looked again, the people hanging on the wall had changed. Now they were fallen soldiers that I'd served with. People I'd been in charge of.

People I'd failed.

Something hard and cold pressed against my temple. Turning away from the sight of my unconscious comrades, I looked up into the eyes of my captor. They were jabbering away in a language I didn't know, and an insane bubble of laughter welled up in my throat.

Talking to me now was pointless. They'd already killed my translator. If they wanted to negotiate, they should have started with that.

Now we were all fucked.

The more questions they shouted at me that I couldn't answer, the angrier they got. I recognized the look in my captor's eyes.

Desperation.

Resignation.

Insanity.

They were beyond reason. Even if we spoke the same language, I wouldn't be able to negotiate with them.

CREED

Staring down the barrel of my captor's gun, I was certain that I was about to die.

A sudden bang echoed in my ears. I flinched, certain that they'd pulled the trigger.

Yet, instead of the pain I expected, there was just more shouting.

Slowly, already dreading what I'd see, I opened my eyes.

I was no longer out in the woods, or in a forgotten basement. Instead, I was inside some sort of vehicle, probably a van or a truck with a large space in the back. My hands were tied behind me, but my legs were free, and I was lying directly on the metal floor.

Reality and dream blurred together, and I wasn't sure what was real anymore. There were no unconscious bodies hanging on the walls, but there was still an enemy shouting angry words. This time I knew the language, but a violent buzzing in my ears kept me from understanding what was being said. The person had Kayden pinned to the wall, shaking him hard enough that his back slammed against the metal.

Awake or dreaming didn't matter. Either way, I was still a captive.

Our enemy kept their face covered by a bandana so only their eyes were visible as they shouted at Kayden. They were different eyes than my captor before, but the look in them was exactly the same.

Fury.

Bloodlust.

A desire to lash out and injure someone.

I'd seen that look far too many times, but this time it wasn't directed at me.

It was directed at Kayden.

I needed to do something. They were going to kill him. My hands were bound, but my legs were free. I should have been able to do something with that.

Yet, all I did was lie there uselessly,

struggling to breathe as I watched our captor slam Kayden against the wall one more time before throwing him to the floor.

"Useless fag," our captor muttered as they stormed off.

It was funny that, out of all the shouting that had been going on, those were the words I was finally able to hear. A small, vulnerable part of me curled up inside my heart, scared and ashamed of being seen. Like a child that had forgotten their lines at the school play and could do nothing but run off the stage to hide.

Our captor's eyes scanned over me for a moment, but almost immediately dismissed me. I was no threat to them in my current state. Shoving me aside with their foot, they walked past me and hopped out of the van, closing the doors behind them.

Kayden and I were alone, but I still couldn't move. It felt like the chains, which were only wrapped around my wrists, had grown to encase my whole body.

"Creed?" Kayden's voice broke the silence.

Something tapped against my leg, and I jumped. My fight or flight mode activated, and my hands strained against their bonds as I tried to reach for a weapon that didn't exist.

My vision started to go gray around the edges, when the sound of Kayden's voice cut through my panic.

"Creed? Creed! Calm down."

His hands were bound just like mine, so he'd tapped me with his foot. Shame crept up the back of my throat. Kayden was safe. There was no reason for me to overreact so badly, but I couldn't stop.

Why couldn't I breathe?

My tongue was lead inside my mouth. No matter how hard I struggled, I couldn't speak. In the end, I managed to make a vague sound to at least let Kayden know I heard him.

There was shifting sound beside me, and soon Kayden's face came into view, closer than it had been before. He'd twisted himself into an awkward position in order to lie down next to me despite his hands being bound to the wall, but his expression showed no signs of discomfort.

A calm, comforting aura radiated around him, practically making him glow in the dim atmosphere of the van.

"Hey, Creed, look at me." His voice was softer than I'd ever heard before. "I think you're having a panic attack."

Panic attack?

No, that couldn't be right. I wasn't the kind of person who panicked. I was the one who remained stoic while everyone else panicked.

"No, Creed, hey, focus on me." I hadn't even realized that my vision had started to blur, until his voice caught my attention again. "Just try to breathe with me. All right? Breathe in. Then out. Just like that."

I followed his instruction, one breath at a time. At first, I could barely get any air into my lungs, but gradually I was able to take deeper and deeper breaths until finally some clarity returned to my vision.

We must have been lying there silently breathing together for longer than I'd thought. During that time, the van had started moving again, taking us to some unknown location.

When I was finally able to breathe without struggling and see straight again, I sat up and leaned heavily against the wall. Kayden scooted as close to me as he could until his shoulder bumped against mine.

"You all right?"

I swallowed heavily, then nodded. "Yeah. Sorry."

"Hey, don't apologize. If there's ever a time to panic, this is it. But, um, I have to ask. A panic attack seems... out of character for you."

Closing my eyes, I laughed weakly under my breath. "That wasn't actually a question."

Kayden stuttered for a moment, trying to figure out what to say, but I cut him off.

"I know what you're trying to ask. I'm the cool-headed one who takes care of business, right? So, something must be wrong if I'm panicking." With a heavy sigh, I resigned myself to a difficult explanation and turned to face him. "First, let me ask you, what do you know about my retirement from the military?"

His brow furrowed as he thought, and I hated the way it cast a shadow over his eyes. Kayden should only ever be smiling.

"I know you retired a bit early because something went wrong with your last mission. Brody and Magnus told me a little about it before we left, but they seemed to imply it wasn't that big of a deal."

My hands itched for something to fidget with. A pen. A stone. An old stick. Anything.

But all I grasped was air.

"I was taken POW on my last mission. Magnus and Brody think I arranged it in order to retire early but... that's a lie. They just assumed and I never corrected them."

Kayden's shoulder pressed more firmly against mine. "So, you actually were..."

He couldn't finish the question, but he didn't need to.

Biting my lip, I nodded.

"I fucked up. I was distracted by everything that was happening with Magnus and Brody and I wasn't paying enough attention. Our enemies got the drop on me during a mission and my whole team was captured. It's a damn miracle most of us were saved as quickly as we were."

Kayden was a professional writer. Words were his literal job. So, of course he picked up on the most important word in my entire explanation.

"Most?"

"Yeah. A few of our guys were killed in the initial capture. One of them was our translator. None of us spoke the native language of the area, and our captors didn't speak English. Without a translator, the whole thing went south real quick. We couldn't even negotiate. I thought..."

Panic started to creep in again, dissolving the edges of my vision into a gray fog. My hands shook against their restraints.

Kayden pressed as close to me as he could, tipping his neck to an uncomfortable angle so his head rested against mine. "It's all right," he said in the same soothing voice he'd used earlier. "Deep breaths. Obviously, you escaped. You don't have to tell me about it if you don't want to, but it's clearly affecting you. I'm guessing that being captured again isn't doing you any favors."

With a growl of frustration, I knocked my head back against the metal wall of the van.

"Damn it. I hate this. I've never been truly helpless before. Even in our worst scrapes and our most dangerous missions, there was always a chance of survival. I could always see a path forward, even if it was difficult or unlikely. But that last mission, while I was staring down the gun and waiting for them to kill me, I couldn't see anything except my own death. After I survived, and I retired, I swore I would never have to feel like that again."

I felt Kayden nod more than I saw the

movement.

"Yet, here you are again."

"Yet, here I am again, in the same damn position, just as helpless as before."

Finally saying it out loud was like lancing an infected wound. It hurt, but there was also a sense of relief. So much rot had built up inside me, every time I let Magnus and Brody continue their assumption that I controlled the whole situation, and every time pushed away my own fear, the infection buried itself deeper.

With the truth finally hanging out in the open air between us, some of the pressure building in my chest over the last few weeks abated and I could breathe a little easier.

"No," I declared with more strength than I felt. "It's not the same. The people who kidnapped me before were professionals. They knew what they were doing. These guys are amateurs at best.

Probably just civilians with a little too much power."

"You're certain?"

"Yeah. Look at us." I wiggled my legs to show off what I meant. "We're only secured by our wrists. A professional would never allow us so much movement or let us stay so close together. Plus, that guy who was in here earlier, he didn't know the first thing about intimidation. He didn't even pull out a weapon to back up his threats."

Kayden shifted uncomfortably. "I don't know, it felt pretty threatening when he was slamming me against the wall."

I leaned some of my weight against him in a show of comfort. "Sorry about that. I shouldn't have let you face that alone."

"It's fine. I was just worried about you. At first you were asleep, but even after you woke up you were completely out of it. Like you were comatose or something.

When that guy came in to question us, I didn't want him to notice the state you were in, so I tried to keep his attention on me." Kayden flinched, and if his hands had been free, he probably would have rubbed at the back of his head. "I think my plan worked a little too well."

"What did they want?"

I probably should have asked that earlier, but I'd been so distracted by everything else that the reason for our capture hadn't seemed as important as the actual capture itself.

To my surprise, Kayden snorted like I'd just told a dumb joke.

"They want the same thing that Deputy who visited you wanted. Lisianthus Milford's journal. They have it, but they can't decipher it either. Just like the Deputy, they want you to crack the code for them."

The van hit a bump, and the two of us jostled together. The chains around our wrists jingled with an almost merry sound, like Christmas bells.

"What makes them so sure I can figure it out?" I asked.

Kayden just shrugged, making his restraints chime again. "That Deputy was pretty certain that you could, so that seems to be a good enough reason for them to also assume that you can. Are they wrong?"

Sighing deeply, I twisted my wrists against the chains until I found the waistband of my pants. Damn, they'd taken my belt. I had a knife hidden in the buckle that might have been helpful. Even if our captors were just a bunch of puffed-up civilians, they were cautious. I had to give them that much.

"I might be able to. I've had some training in code breaking, but it's not my specialty."

"Don't let them hear you say that, or they'll have no reason to keep us around."

Kayden started laughing. The sound was more manic than joyful, making it clear that he didn't find the situation humorous. He laughed simply because he didn't know what else to do.

Still, being reminded of how helpless we were wasn't pleasant. My expression grew grim, and I clenched my hands into tight fists.

Noticing my reaction, Kayden silenced his laughter. "Sorry, I shouldn't joke like that."

"No," I shook my head. "It's fine. Do whatever you need to in order to stay calm. I'm going to need you."

"Need me?" Kayden snorted like he was about to laugh again but cut himself off. "I don't think so. I can't help you break a code, and I've never even been in a fight before. There's nothing I can do to help. I'm just a liability here."

"No, you've very important," I insisted. I really wished I could reach out to him.

Hold his hand, cup his face, anything to demonstrate how serious I was. "Giving them what they want doesn't guarantee we'll survive. Our best bet is to bide our time and plan our escape. I'm going to get us out of here, I promise, but I'll need your help. If I start to panic again, I'll need you to calm me down and keep me focused, just like you did a few minutes ago. Think you can do it?"

With a determined expression on his face, he nodded. "I'd do it even if we weren't in danger. I hate seeing you panic like that."

Shifting in place, I managed to angle my body in a way that allowed me to press a light kiss to the corner of his mouth.

"All right. I'm going to get us out of here. Trust me?"

He returned my kiss with one of his own.

"I trust you."

CREED

***

Without a clock it was impossible to tell the exact time, but I guessed it was about another half hour before the van came to a stop. I tried to coach Kayden on what to expect, so neither of us were too surprised when our captors placed dark bags over our heads before leading us out of the van. They were being careful not to give us any clues about our location.

That meant there was something worth noticing. My hope was that we'd eventually be able to get a good look at our surroundings, because right now, I had no clue where we were. There was no telling how long we'd been unconscious, so we could very well have been taken to the other side of the country.

With our heads completely covered, neither Kayden nor I could walk very well. A strong hand gripped each of my arms, half leading me and half dragging me along. Based on the sounds around us that I could barely make out through the bag, it seemed like they brought us inside a building. Whispers followed us, not close enough for me to hear what they were saying, but enough to know that we were surrounded by many people.

Fighting our way out wouldn't be possible. For now, we'd have to play along with what they wanted and wait for an opportunity.

Unfortunately, there were two of us. If Kayden was right and they wanted me to crack the code on Lisianthus Milford's journal, then I was the only one they needed. Kayden was expendable.

Eventually, we were brought to a stop, and someone kicked the back of my knees, forcing me to kneel. The landing was soft. I was kneeling on a thick carpet. Wherever we were, this wasn't some forgotten basement out in the middle of nowhere.

Hopefully, the setting was different enough that it wouldn't trigger any unwanted memories.

We were left waiting for several long minutes, hands bound, completely blind and mostly deaf.

The definition of helpless.

There was no warning before the bags were suddenly removed from our heads. One minute my vision was shrouded in black, and the next bright light assaulted my eyes. I wanted to blink, shake my head, or do something to help clear my vision, but that would only make me look vulnerable. Instead, I kept my expression calm as I waited for my eyes to adjust, pretending that I could see clearly the entire time.

"So, you're the one whose been giving us so much trouble?" a voice said.

I could just see the vague outline of a person standing a few feet away. If not for the voice, I wouldn't have even been able to tell if they were a man or a woman.

Rolling my eyes, I put on my most irritating smile. The one that used to make both teachers and bullies hate me as a child. It hadn't been intentional when I was younger. According to Kayden, my "face just wasn't built for smiling" so the expression always looked insincere on me.

Now, I used it to my advantage.

"You must be mistaken. I only arrived about a week ago."

My vision finally cleared enough for me to see who I was talking to. The man had a clean-cut look, like a pastor, but there was just a little too much muscle under his tailored clothes. This was not a man who sat around all day preaching.

The man glared at me but didn't come any closer. "Don't try to be funny. Your friends may have started this, but you were there when several of our members were arrested."

I pretended to think for a moment,

which likely only pissed our captors off more, but it gave me a chance to cast a quick glance over at Kayden. He was obviously afraid, but he was doing a good job keeping himself together. His face was neutral, and only the stiff set of his shoulders and the way he bit his lip to silence himself gave away the fact that he was terrified.

"Oh, was that you?" I said, feigning nonchalance as I shrugged. "Sorry. I didn't realize. What was your name again? Something about souls, right? The Tired Souls? No, that's not right. The Trained Souls?"

"Shut up!" the other man snapped. He took a step forward as if he meant to approach me, but then stopped and regained his place on the other side of the room.

That was when I realized the man wasn't alone. There were other people in the room behind me, that much I could tell even without seeing them, but there was someone else directly in front of me as well. The second man sat at a small but elaborate desk, reminding me of the way that a king would sit on a throne while holding court. He was very old, his sparse hair completely white, and the wrinkles on his face too numerous to count. The way he sat there, not saying a word and barely moving, made it seem like he wasn't paying attention, but his eyes were very active as he tracked the activity around the room.

The younger man shouting at me may pretend to be the one in charge of this little cult, but the older man was the real leader.

That's who I needed to watch out for.

The man who'd shouted at me laid a hand on the back of the chair of the man sitting down. Just that little gesture was enough to calm him down, and he spoke to me in a much more level tone.

"Mister Landry. Let's not play these games. We both know why you're here."

I wasn't going to give him the satisfaction of giving him the answers he was looking for.

"We're here because you kidnapped us."

The younger man—I really wished they'd introduce themselves, so I'd have some names for them—squeezed the back of the older man's chair. His knuckles turned white, like he was on the verge of losing control again, but he managed to keep himself calm.

"We're here because your friends discovered the missing body of our late founder. Generations ago, something important was stolen from him. It was so important that he gave up his life trying to retrieve it. The items your friends found with his body are likely the key to getting back what was stolen. For that, we need your help. The locket and the key have already revealed their secrets, but the information stored in the journal continues to elude us. You have skills that will help with that."

So, we'd reached the negotiation stage of our kidnapping. At least things were going better than the last time I'd been captured.

This time, everyone spoke the same language.

"I have no connection to you or the Milford sisters. The only reason I'm involved in this at all is that my friends and I were unlucky enough to buy a property that had a coffin buried in it. So, what's in it for me if I help you?"

The younger man was clearly furious over my continued attitude, but it was the older man's reaction that caught my interest. He'd clearly been paying attention to everything, but up until that moment he had given off a sense of indifference. When I mentioned the

Milford sisters, however, his expression shifted. Just for a moment, the wrinkles of his face tightened and twisted into a look of absolute disgust.

Whatever the younger man was saying, I ignored him and turned my attention fully on the older man.

"You. What's your name?"

The young man, and everyone else in the room stationed behind me, gasped as if I'd just spit in their face.

The older man, however, just laughed quietly.

"An observant boy, aren't you."

His voice was rough but flowing, like a river of sand.

"Your reaction is different from everyone else's," I explained. "This is personal for you. But these events happened a hundred and twenty-five years ago. For you to have a personal connection to those events, there's only a few options."

The man adjusted something just below the table, and a moment later, I could hear the whirr of a machinery. He glided out from behind the desk in an electric wheelchair.

The young man reached out as if to stop the man in the chair from getting any closer. "Father, wait, you don't have to."

"Nonsense," the older man cut him off. "I'm not so old that I can't even handle one conversation. Besides, Mister Landry here is a respectable man. He deserves to know the importance of what he's found himself involved in."

The wheels of his chair rolled slowly over the carpet, stopping just a few feet in front of me.

"My name is Chester Grieve. Angus Grieve, our founder, was my great-uncle. Obviously, I never knew him personally, but my grandfather did, and he told me about the man. This is not just a matter of our community's history, but it is about my family's legacy."

"So, the Milford sisters stole something from your great-uncle."

"Milford." Chester Grieve spat the word between his teeth, like a cherry pit that he'd nearly swallowed. "Even in death, all these years later, they continue to mock us. The name of those unfaithful harlots isn't Milford. It's Grieve. They were our founder's wives. He gave them the honor of marrying them, and they upheld their vows by betraying him."

Before I could say anything in response, Kayden suddenly interrupted.

"Wait. All three of them?"

He'd been so quiet up until now that most people had forgotten he was even in the room, but now he had everyone's attention. His shoulders hunched and he slouched where he knelt, clearly regretting that he'd spoken at all.

I wished he'd remained quiet, but I

couldn't blame him for his shock.

Determined to get everyone's attention off of Kayden and back onto myself, I laughed with the harshest sound I could muster. "Your founder married a set of triplets? What? Was one not enough for him?"

Chester Grieve clenched his jaw so hard that his aged teeth were in danger of shattering to dust. "It is an honor to be chosen as the leader's wife. It was their job to help lead our community, and they abandoned that duty."

I cut my laughter off abruptly, and gave the old man the most disgusted look I could muster. "I was told that those sisters were only teenagers when they were taken in by the Milford family. Your founder certainly had an... *interesting* taste in wives. Your little cult was founded by a pedophile and based on the number of times you've tried to kill the people I care about; I doubt you're much better. So, why would I help you?"

The metallic click of a gun sounded behind us. Kayden flinched, and I felt the buzzing of familiar panic stabbing at the edges of my mind.

Before the gun-wielder stepped into view, Chester Grieve waved them away. The threat was clear even if they didn't point the weapon at us directly.

"It's simple. If you don't help us, then we'll kill your friend here." He said the word "friend" with almost as much disgust as he said the name "Milford". The cult had probably been following us for a while and must have seen me with Kayden. They knew how important he was to me.

I had a decision to make. I already knew I was going to give in to their demands, at least until I could figure out a way to escape. However, if I gave in too easily, it wouldn't be believable, and I'd only make them more suspicious.

How much resistance was enough?

Remembering the number of gun fights and other life-threatening conflicts that Magnus and Brody had with these people, I guessed that their expectations of resistance were pretty high.

Squaring my shoulders, I hoped that Kayden would recognize my act for what it was.

"Do you think such a little threat is enough to control me? I've been threatened by enemies much more intimidating than you, from all over the world. You aren't even the first ones to take me captive. I didn't give in to their demands then, what makes you think I'd give into you so easily."

Chester Grieve also wasn't a man so easily intimidated. Despite sitting in a wheelchair, he held his ground.

"We've done our research on you, Creed Landry. You're an accomplished soldier, a talented pilot, and a determined survivalist. You're also an honorable man. This man here is important to you, and despite the stoic face you put on, the guilt of causing his death would eat away at you, and you know it."

The old man's eyes had a slightly milky quality to their color, a sign of his advanced age, but his gaze was still sharp.

Every nerve in my body burned with the urge to lash out at him as I stared into his eyes.

"You're right. I won't deny that. But let me warn you, if you kill him, then there is nothing you can do, no torture on this earth, that will make me help you."

Like two predators locked in a battle for the last piece of territory, we stared each other down in silence. I refused to flinch, even as the rest of the world turned gray and muted around me. My vision tunneled, until all I could see were those cold, cloudy eyes staring back at me.

Chester Grieve broke first and looked away.

"Take them somewhere to rest for a bit," he instructed the others in the room. "Our guests have had a long journey, and Mister Landry here needs time to think over my proposal."

Immediately, the black bags were shoved back over our heads, and we were hauled to our feet. More hands shoved at us, leading us out of the room to whatever prison they had planned for us.

Despite the rough manhandling, a sense of pride swelled up inside my chest.

This time, I'd won.

CHAPTER SIX

Kayden

TWO DAYS.

We'd been held captive for two days. Locked in a small, windowless room, there was no sunlight to show us the passing days, but there was a clock to mark each second that ticked by.

At least there was a bed. When we'd been dragged off, I'd feared these crazy cult people would lock us in a dungeon of some sort, but it was just a regular room. Small, and likely underground, based on the staircase we'd been brought down to get here, but a normal room otherwise.

I sat on the bed and leaned against the wall as I watched Creed work at the desk in the corner. The room had very little furniture, literally just the bed and the desk. It was barely big enough for one person, let alone two, so although Creed was technically across the room from me, he was still close enough for me to reach out and touch if I wanted.

He'd agreed to decipher the journal for the cult leader. There wasn't really another choice, unless either of us suddenly turned suicidal. Even when Creed had stood up to the cult leader, acting like he wouldn't give in to the old man's demands, I knew it had been an act. Playing along with what they wanted was our only means of survival.

Still, it had been terrifying, and I'd bitten the inside of my cheek until I tasted blood to keep myself silent during the nerve-wracking moment when Creed had been staring the leader down.

Now he sat hunched over a table, pouring over the papers spread across its surface. The cult hadn't trusted him with the original journal but had instead given him copied photos of all the pages.

For hours at a time, Creed just sat there, constantly scribbling on a notepad. I had no idea what he was doing, but based on his frustration he didn't seem to be making any progress.

Over the last two days, my fear had quickly given way to boredom. There was nothing to do but stare at the blank walls while Creed worked.

Curious, and with nothing better to do, I waited until I noticed Creed's pen stop scratching over the paper and left the bed to stand beside him.

"Any luck?"

Creed leaned back in his chair, making the old wood groan, and stretched his arms above his head until his back made an audible crack.

"No sudden breakthroughs, if that's what you're asking."

I picked up the notepad, looking over what he'd been writing. It looked like the same gibberish that filled the journal.

"What exactly are you doing?"

With a heavy sigh, Creed threw his pen down onto the table.

"Well, with these kinds of things there's generally two ways to crack a code. The first is to study the author and figure out what kind of code they would use, and they probably would have written about so that you know what you're looking for. Unfortunately, this author has been dead for nearly a century, and nothing is known about this journal, so that's not an option."

"So, what's the second option?"

He looked up at me with a tired grin. "Brute force. I keep trying different methods until something works."

"But..." I turned my gaze back to the pages and pages of nonsense letters. "That could take forever."

"Not if you know where to start." He pointed at one of the pages lying on top of the pile. "Small words, with only one or two letters, are the key. Assuming this is written in English, only two words are spelled with a single letter. 'I' and 'A'. Plus, there's also only twenty-four commonly used two letter words. So, I make an assumption on what the word is supposed to be, and work backward to figure out what kind of code would result in the letters found on the page. Then I take that code and see if it works on any other words. Rinse and repeat until I find an answer."

So far, despite all the pages that Creed had filled with writing, I still wasn't seeing any words.

"So, are you close?"

"Nope." He picked the pen back up, tossing it in the air a few times before pulling over a new sheet of blank paper. "I think the author might have used multiple layers of codes, or different codes for different types of words, but I'm going to finish writing out all the possible options first before moving on to other ideas."

The desk only had one chair, so I threw myself back onto the bed rather than continue standing around.

"Why? If you know you aren't on the right track, why keep plugging away on an idea that isn't working."

Creed's pen hovered just over the surface of the blank paper without touching it.

"Because the longer this takes me, the longer we can stall for time to figure out a way out of here."

My mood instantly dimmed. I'd almost forgotten why we were really here. For now, we were safe so long as it seemed like Creed was giving them what they wanted, but the cult would only wait so long.

And if Creed did succeed at cracking the code and deciphering the journal, then they would have no reason to continue keeping us alive.

The scratching of Creed's pen on paper was the only sound that filled the room for several minutes. Each new letter that he wrote set my teeth more and more on edge until it felt like my nerves had been twisted into corkscrews. I wanted to scream and bang my head against the wall, but when I finally managed to open my mouth, my voice came out incredibly small.

"I'm sorry."

The sound of Creed's pen stopped.

"What the hell are you talking about?"

I rolled over on the bed, so I was facing the opposite wall away from him. "You're only here because of me."

For a minute there was nothing but silence, but then wood scraped against wood as Creed pushed his chair away from the table. A moment later, the bed dipped and Creed lay down behind me. His arm wrapped around my waist and his nose pressed against the back of my neck.

"I repeat, what the hell are you talking about?"

Even under these circumstances, I couldn't resist the urge to turn around so I could get a better view of Creed. I'd pined after the man for so many years, that being able to hold him and be held by him still felt like a dream.

"You only got captured because I dragged you off into the woods for a dumb camping trip. If I hadn't been so selfish, you'd be back safe in the home you were building with your friends."

Our foreheads pressed together, and

Creed bumped his head against me just hard enough for it to feel like a reprimand. "Brody and Magnus have both been attacked, and even captured, several times already. Sitting safely at home is no guarantee that nothing would happen, especially with determined enemies like this. Besides, it wasn't dumb. It was for your job."

Dipping my head down, I buried my face under his chin so I wouldn't have to look directly at him.

"No, it wasn't. I told you before, remember? My publisher wanted to send me somewhere else. I only begged them to let me take a domestic trip, so I had an excuse to come see you."

"Oh, right."

Creed's voice had an awkward hitch to it, and for a moment I thought I'd made him uncomfortable, but when I tried to pull away, he just held me tighter.

"Kay?" The sound of my nickname on

his lips made me shudder. He spoke those three letters as if he were tasting them, and it felt almost as intimate as a kiss. "I meant to ask this earlier, but when you first told me why you actually came out here, it sounded like you'd been interested in me for a while."

I sighed and pressed closer against his chest. If he was going to continue offering physical comfort, then I was going to keep lapping it up for as long as I could.

"Yeah," I admitted. "I've been... Well, there's no easy way to say it, but I've been in love with you for a long time."

I thought he would question the word love. After all, it had only been a few days since my confession. I'd been obsessing over Creed for years, so love was an easy word to use, but for Creed this must all feel like it was happening very fast.

However, he surprised me. Instead of fixating on the word "love" like I'd expected, he instead latched on to a different part of my admission.

"A long time? How long, exactly?"

I tried to just shrug and play it off like I didn't know the answer, but Creed didn't accept that. He called me by my nickname again, using that same intimate tone of voice that filled me with warmth all the way down to my toes, and I was helpless to keep anything from him.

"I guess I always kinda had feelings for you, but I knew for certain that I was in love with you when I was fifteen."

Drawing back to put some space between us, Creed tipped up my chin, so I had to look at him.

"Your fifteenth birthday party?"

I cringed. "You remember that?"

"I remember you threw a fit. I didn't remember why you were upset, but you said that I was a terrible friend and then didn't talk to me for two weeks."

I desperately wanted to look away from him, but he still held my chin, so I was forced to face him.

"You brought that girl from our class as a date to the party. I wanted to die inside, watching her sit on your lap like she belonged there. It took all my self-control not to drag her off of you by the hair."

Dark eyes opened wide as Creed gaped at me. "That's why? Fuck, I don't even remember her name. What was it... Cindy? Carol? I don't know. We dated for like, two weeks. The only thing worse than dating her was trying to break up with her." Creed suddenly stopped talking for a moment, and I could practically see the lightbulb flash to life in his eyes as he made a connection. "Oh, that's why you started talking to me again."

"Don't remind me," I mumbled. My face burned with embarrassment as I recalled the childish actions of my teenage self. "God, I was a mess when I was younger. Still am, but now I can at least hide it better. Younger me was a jealous little monster."

Creed laughed and kissed my forehead. "I don't mind. I was a mess back then, too. But that's actually what I'm curious about. How did you know?"

"Know what?"

"That you were gay. You knew back when you were fifteen. How did you figure it out so quickly and how were you able to accept it? It took me forever to figure it out, and even now I'm still not that comfortable admitting it out loud. How did you do it?"

All I could do was shrug. "I don't know. It was always just such a clear part of me, there was no point trying to deny it. As for how I was so comfortable admitting I was gay... I hate to say it, but the only person whose opinion I cared about was you. And you were so oblivious back then, I probably could have kissed you full on the mouth and you wouldn't have realized what that mean. Other than that, I didn't care if anyone else knew."

This was one of the few topics we'd never really discussed, but even now, I could tell what Creed was thinking as his eyes darted around, looking for answers that weren't there.

Wrapping a hand around his head in a firm grip, I pulled him into a deep kiss, effectively silencing the complex thoughts that had undoubtedly been building inside his head. The kiss lasted for several minutes, long enough to be sure that I had his full attention, but I pulled back just enough to speak.

"You know, it's okay that it took you a while to figure yourself out. There's no time limit for these things."

"I know." Creed nodded. "But I can't help but think, if I'd been able to come to terms with it earlier, if I'd been able to admit that I was... gay, then we could have had a lot more time together."

CREED

I couldn't help it. I had to kiss him again. It was a much briefer exchange, but I poured as much emotion into it as I could.

"Oh, you silly, sentimental man. I love you. You know that? Maybe it's too early to say, but I do."

I watched as Creed hesitated as his own words stuck in his throat. Love was such a heavy word. He wasn't ready to say it back to me yet, but that was all right. I was patient.

I'd waited this long already just to be able to admit my feelings for him. I could wait a little longer to finally hear them back.

The awkward moment was saved by a knock at the door. Creed and I both quickly stood from the bed, not wanting to be caught in an awkward position. The door only locked from the outside. While we couldn't leave, anyone could just walk in at any time.

Luckily, the person on the other side waited for us to give the okay before even trying the handle. The young boy who opened the door had become familiar to us over the last few days. His name was Robyn, and he was by far the most pleasant part of this whole kidnapping fiasco. He always greeted us with a smile, and this time was no exception as he held up a tray.

"I've got food for you guys. Sorry it's the same stuff as yesterday and, well, every meal. They won't let me bring you anything else."

Creed cleared some of his papers off the table so Robyn could set down the tray, presenting us our meager lunch of soup and bread.

Despite being only around twelve years old, Robyn was in charge of bringing us all our meals. After we'd first been locked in this room, one of the adult cult members had brought us our meals, but that had quickly turned sour when they tried to take the opportunity to threaten us. The ensuing scuffle had left Creed with a black eye, and the cult member with a broken arm.

Now, they sent us a child to bring us our meals instead, rightfully assuming that we wouldn't attack someone so young.

"How's your sister?" I asked the boy as I grabbed one of the bowls for myself. There was only one chair, which I let Creed have, so I awkwardly remained standing to eat. "Is she still sick?"

"Mavis's cold is getting better," Robyn said while fetching our bowls from the previous meal, which we'd stashed in the corner of the room. "She should be back on her feet soon, and then I'll be busy again chasing after her."

Apparently, the children's mother had died in childbirth with the young sister. They'd been raised by their father until about a year ago when the man had died due to some disease that Robyn didn't fully understand. That left the twelve-year-old boy to take care of his six-year-old sister all by himself.

I'd tried asking once why none one else in their "community" could take them in, but Robyn had given me such an evasive answer that I decided never to try asking again. Whatever politics were going on inside the cult were none of my business.

Robyn clutched the old tray in front of him like a shield, staring down at his shoes like they he was holding a conversation with them instead of us.

"Um, do you think, once Mavis's cold is gone, I could bring her to meet you? I've told her all about our guests, and she's really curious about you. She's never met anyone outside our community before."

I shared a look with Creed. Neither of us had much experience with children, but between the two of us, I was at least better at talking to people. There was an unspoken agreement between us to let me handle the awkward conversations.

The only question was, should we be blunt with our answer, or should we let the kid down easy?

For the sake of caution, I decided to try the easy approach.

"Creed and I wouldn't mind meeting her. Your sister sounds lovely. However, I don't think the rest of your community would agree, and we don't want you to get in trouble."

Robyn didn't push it any farther, just silently nodded to himself. He was young, but he was old enough to understand what was going on, and he probably knew that even asking to bring his sister to meet us was already crossing a line.

"I have to get going," he said as he headed for the door. "I have a lot of chores to do. I'll bring you your diner later."

The door clicked softly behind him. Its

lock was unobtrusive but impenetrable. As usual, Creed checked the door just to see if we could open it, but the handle wouldn't even budge. When we'd first been locked in here, he'd tried breaking the door down, but only succeeded in bruising his shoulder. It looked like wood, but that was just a façade, and it was actually reinforced with metal.

Our room looked ordinary, if a bit dim due to the lack of windows, but it was an effective prison.

Shaking his head, Creed went back to the table.

"Joining a cult is one thing. Adults can make that choice for themselves if they want, but being born into a cult is an entirely different matter. Those kids didn't choose this kind of isolated life."

I stirred the spoon in my bowl, not even seeing the soup in front of me. "Without being exposed to the broader world, they may not even realize they have a choice." No longer hungry, I set the bowl aside. "There are so many things I didn't understand until I started traveling around, and I at least knew there was a bigger world out there for me. I can't imagine what it'd be like if I didn't even know that traveling was an option."

"Not to mention making that kid raise his little sister on his own. It's no wonder the Milford sisters chose to escape. I'm surprised more people don't try to leave."

"Even if they wanted to leave, they may not be able to," I reminded him.

Creed just grunted in agreement. His attention was already back on his papers, and he was scribbling away on his notepad with one hand while spooning soup into his mouth with the other. The soup was bland and unappetizing, but Creed had made a point of explaining how important it was that we keep our strength up. Starving ourselves only made things easier for our captors.

My own bowl sat untouched, making me feel guilty over the wasted food, but I just couldn't bring myself to eat. My stomach was twisted up in knots, and if I tried to eat anything, I'd probably just make myself nauseous.

Time continued to tick by slowly as Creed's pen continued its work. I dozed off at some point, drifting between conscious and dreaming like skimming across the surface of ocean waves.

I was startled awake some time later by a harsh knock on the door.

That clearly wasn't Robyn. The boy always knocked with a polite little tapping sound, not this loud bang that seemed in danger of taking the door off its hinges.

This person also didn't wait for our permission to enter. Almost as soon as they finished knocking, the door slammed open.

"You fuckers decent?"

No, this was not Robyn at all. It took

me a moment to recognize the man who now stood in the room. He was related to Chester Grieve, and although he acted like he was the cult leader, he was basically his father's lackey.

He didn't wait for an answer to his rude question before heading over to Creed's worktable.

"What progress have you made?"

"I haven't cracked the code, if that's what you want to know."

Creed had been on his feet the moment there was a knock on the door, and he now glared at the other man who was sifting through the papers.

"This just looks like more drivel. Are you really doing anything?"

Snatching the papers from the man, Creed placed them back on the table in order. "I'm not going to bother explaining it to you. Do you actually need anything?"

The man pulled two familiar black bags out of his pocket. "My father wants to speak with you."

It was almost routine now, having the bags placed over our heads before we were hauled out the door and moved somewhere else. This time, I managed to pay a little more attention to where we were going and based on the size of the staircase leading from the door, it confirmed my suspicion that our room was underground.

Outside in the fresh air, I could hear more sounds of life. There were people nearby, whispering just out of earshot. I felt their presence like the glow of hot coals.

Most telling, however, was the lack of sound. Even outside, I didn't hear any of the noise one would expect in a big city, like the rumble of traffic, the wail of an ambulance in the distance, or the ding of a shop door opening. If anything, this place sounded similar to Creed's home, just a few buildings mostly surrounded by nature.

Wherever we were, it must be remote. Probably just some little spot out in the middle of the wilderness where the cult had carved out a living for itself.

I didn't need Creed's expertise to tell me that our location would make escaping even harder.

We weren't taken very far. Based on the number of steps I took, there couldn't have been more than fifty feet from our prison to our new location. After being led up another staircase and through several doors, I was unceremoniously shoved around until the backs of my legs bumped against something soft and I instinctively sat down. I found myself seated on a very comfortable couch. Creed joined me a moment later, forced to sit on the couch beside me, and then the bags were removed from our heads.

Once again, Chester Grieve sat before us in his wheelchair.

The first time we'd met him in a plain, undistinguishable room. Aside from the carpet, it would have looked no different than a storage room.

This time, however, we were clearly in a more regularly used room. There was art on the walls—vague religious images I didn't recognize—and the furniture was made more for comfort than function.

On the table next to the cult leader was a stack of folders and other various papers. He was reading through one of them, not even looking up to acknowledge us.

I was about to open my mouth and demand to know why he'd brought us here, when Creed grabbed my leg just above the knee. The slight squeeze of his fingers was a clear message for silence.

At least this time our hands weren't bound like they'd been before. Several men armed with impressively large guns stood near the door, blocking the only exit. Escape wasn't possible, but the freedom to move my arms was still an improvement.

If Chester Grieve wanted to continue pretending that we weren't there in some sort of weird power play, I was happy to let him continue sitting there as long as he wanted. I was in no hurry to go back to our small, oppressive room.

Eventually, when it was clear that neither Creed nor I would speak first, the cult leader finally set aside whatever he was reading.

"They tell me you haven't made any progress with the journal."

He only addressed Creed, not even sparing me a glance.

Creed openly scoffed. "If that's what your people told you, then they're idiots."

Insulting the people who literally held our lives in their hands seemed like a bad idea, and I swallowed down the fear that bubbled up in my chest. Creed's hand squeezed my leg again, offering a small gesture of comfort. He seemed completely confident, so I had to assume he knew what he was doing.

"I've made progress," Creed went on to explain. "I just don't have an answer to give you yet."

For a moment, it looked like Chester Grieve wanted to get angry, but then he took a deep breath and right before our eyes the man settled back into a calm focus.

"Never mind that. You've still got time to break the code for us. I trust that you're working hard."

The "or else" at the end of his statement went unspoken, but it was still heard by everyone in the room.

Creed still never wavered and met the cult leader's gaze without flinching.

"If you didn't bring us here to discuss the journal, then what do you want?"

Picking up the top folder from the

stack near him, Chester Grieve started flipping through it again.

"I want to talk about you, Mister Landry. Your mother was Beatrice Landry, maiden name Sherwood, and your father was Arthur Landry. You were an average student with no real prospects growing up until you decided to join the military right out of high school. Since then, you've received many awards and accolades for your service. Several of your missions have earned you some impressive medals, including the Purple Heart. Is that correct?"

I felt Creed's hand tense on my leg. He still looked calm on the outside, but I could tell that Chester Grieve suddenly rattling off information about his life shook him.

"You've done your research about me," he said, biting the words as much as saying them. "Why? You already knew I was a soldier. What good will knowing my parents' names do you?"

"Not much," Chester Grieve sighed as he closed the folder. "You've barely spoken to your parents, or any of your family, since you left for the service. But I'm curious about one thing."

He leaned forward as far as his wheelchair would allow.

"Why would a man with plenty of living family, and even a dear friend waiting for you, choose to buy a random patch of land that he has no connection to?"

CHAPTER SEVEN

Creed

WHILE KAYDEN AND I had been locked away together, I hadn't just been trying to crack the code to Lisianthus's journal. I'd also been preparing myself for the inevitable interrogation we would face. A man like Chester Grieve would only be so patient. Sooner or later, he'd demand answers from us.

I had mentally run through every question and interrogation tactic I thought he would use and composed answers beforehand.

I thought I'd prepared for any possibility.

I was wrong.

Out of all things that the man could have asked, I never expected him to question why Magnus, Brody, and I had purchased our property in Emberwood.

There was no point in even trying to bluff an answer when I had no idea what he was looking for.

"I... don't understand the question," I was forced to admit.

Chester Grieve idly waved a folder that was probably filled with pages of information about me.

"I've looked into it. Neither you nor your companions have any ties to the area. No family nearby, and by all accounts, none of you have even visited the state, let alone ever set foot in Emberwood before."

"So what?"

CREED

Cold eyes, frosted with their advanced age, regarded me without a hint of human emotion. A robot would have had more life in its gaze.

I'd seen that look on only a few people before. Those who were so hopeless they had nothing left in them, and those who were so sure in their convictions there was no room in them for anything else.

Chester Grieve was many things, but he was not hopeless.

"It just strikes me as odd," he continued to say as if we were merely having a casual conversation. "I can understand if you didn't want to live near family. Not all families are... harmonious, after all. But of all the random mountain towns in the country, why Emberwood?"

I recalled the day Magnus, Brody, and I had first discovered the property listing. We'd been randomly looking through real estate sites in our spare time, mostly just trying to figure out what we even wanted.

Until then, we'd had a vague list of requirements, such as the amount of land we thought we could handle, and a price point we were comfortable with, but other than that, everything had been up in the air.

The idea of building our homes from scratch hadn't occurred to us, until we randomly stumbled across the listing in Emberwood.

From the moment we saw it, something about the place just felt right. Plans for what we could do with the land fell into place as if we'd been discussing them for months. We could already tell exactly where Magnus's garden would go, and where Brody would put his workshop.

But how could I possibly explain this to Chester Grieve?

The man was expecting a concrete answer, and I had none.

"We just... liked the place," I eventually

said.

I expected Chester Grieve to get angry over my lack of a proper answer; even to my own ears it felt like I was deflecting.

Instead, however, a smile spread across his face.

"You just liked the place? How very... sentimental."

"Is there a point to this?" I snapped. Something about the man's tone sent an unpleasant feeling snaking up my spine. The way he looked at me made me feel like a display in a museum, like I'd been unearthed against my will and given meaning that even I didn't understand.

After a moment, Chester Grieve relented, and he sat back in his wheelchair in a more relaxed pose.

"I just wanted to check up on your progress. The contents of that journal are very important to us, and I want to make sure you're giving it your full attention. No..." His eyes flickered over to Kayden.

"Unnecessary distractions."

I tensed, ready to fight if the man even suggested removing Kayden from me. However, surprisingly, Kayden stayed relaxed at my side. When I gave him a brief glance of my own, I found his brow furrowed, lost in thought. He hadn't even noticed Chester Grieve's hinted threat.

Before I could ask him what was wrong—or more likely steer the conversation in a different direction—Kayden spoke up.

"Actually, what is the point of this?"

The wheelchair creaked as Chester Grieve rolled a little closer. "The point is for you to solve the journal. That shouldn't be hard to understand."

Realizing the ire that he'd drawn to himself, Kayden squirmed in his seat, nervously eyeing the armed men by the door.

"I know, but, um... this is all because the Milford sis— I mean, your founder's wives stole something from him when they escaped?"

"They didn't escape," Chester Grieve said through gritted teeth, properly paying attention to Kayden for the first time since we'd been kidnapped. "They abandoned their duty."

"Right..." Kayden nodded, though he clearly didn't agree. I tried to silently signal Kayden to be quiet, but he kept talking. "It's just, you don't even know what they stole, or if the journal will even help you. This seems like a lot of effort, you know, kidnapping us and everything, just to find some unknown object."

Watching Chester Grieve's reaction, something clicked in my mind, like a gear I hadn't realized was stuck finally started turning.

"You do know."

Those three words were enough to get Chester Grieve's focus off Kayden and back onto me. I intended to keep it that way, so although this would usually be a situation where I kept my thoughts to myself, I voiced them out loud to make sure I had the man's full attention.

"You know what the sisters stole. That's why you're so determined to find it. Although, you clearly haven't told anyone else. I wonder if your people would be so supportive if they knew what this is really about?"

"It is about justice and righting a wrong that was done to this community over a hundred years ago," Chester Grieve snapped while gesturing at the men standing guard by the door. "Take these two back to their room. I don't want to hear another word about them until they finally have some answers for us."

With guns pointed at us the whole time, a pair of very familiar bags were shoved onto our heads, and rough hands hauled us out of the room.

It was exactly the same as every other

time they'd had to move us, with one notable exception.

There was a small hole in the bag on my head.

It had probably gone unnoticed due to the black fabric. A hole this small wouldn't normally make much of a difference but it just happened to be positioned perfectly for me to see out of it with one eye.

I kept my head down, staring at my feet and letting myself be jostled around to hide the fact that I could see.

The wooden floorboards were old and scuffed, with dust so tightly packed into the grooves between the planks it could never be fully removed. Effort had been made to keep the floors in good condition, they were clean and there were numerous rugs dotted around, but nothing could hide the fact that it was old.

If this was where their leader lived, then the rest of the buildings must be in even worse condition.

That gave me hope. The room where we were being kept wasn't a proper prison. It was just a basement room with a particularly stout lock. Old buildings had weaknesses that could be exploited.

I only needed one opportunity.

Once we stepped outside, I was momentarily blinded by the sight of sunlight. It wasn't even a very bright day, more overcast than blue, but it had been days since I'd seen natural light, and my eyes needed a moment to adjust.

There were more buildings than I thought there'd be. The cult had built themselves a proper little village out in the woods. Yet, the more I looked, the more my suspicions grew. Many of the buildings were in serious disrepair, and few had clearly been abandoned. There also wasn't as much human activity as the number of buildings would suggest.

The cult may have been a thriving

community once, but they were beyond their glory days now. They probably only had half the numbers they used to have.

It was still more people than I could fight on my own. Based on the number of buildings that were still obviously in use, I estimated their numbers to be between sixty and a hundred. If even just half of those people were able-bodied and capable of wielding a weapon, that was a significant fighting force.

We couldn't fight our way out. We'd have to sneak.

I tried to memorize as much of the layout of the buildings as I could. If Kayden and I escaped, we'd need to know where to go.

Though, that still left the question of how we would escape.

A glint of metal in the meager sunlight caught my eye. A few feet in front of us, near a particularly old and crumbling building, a nail lay in the dirt. It was a thick black thing, probably made from solid iron, with an unusually rough quality like it had been made by an inexperienced blacksmith.

That could be useful, if only I could get my hands on it.

Unlike before, this time my hands weren't tied. There might be a chance.

As we came abreast of the nail, I made a show of stumbling over a loose stone. It was a difficult line to walk, making sure that my "fumble" was enough to get a reaction, but not so large that it looked fake.

The man holding me gripped my arm hard enough to bruise and yanked me back upright.

"Keep moving."

I pulled back against their grip.

"Shove me one more time. See what happens."

Of course, how could any man, especially one so comfortable with taking others hostage, ignore such a challenge.

The man shoved me again, harder this time. I could have kept my balance by shifting my weight on my feet, but instead I let myself fall.

Even with the hole in the bag, I still couldn't see very well. It was a hard landing that roughly jarred my shoulder. My hands scrapped across the ground, nicked by small stones and other debris.

Someone's boot planted itself on my back, pressing me down into the soil.

"Fucking idiot. Not much of a soldier, are you? Get up already."

The boot on my back squeezed the air out of my lungs but I still managed to cough out a few words.

"And how... am I... supposed to do that with you standing on me?"

Multiple voices grumbled as hands grabbed me and dragged me to my feet.

Not far away, Kayden was looking around blindly with the bag still on his head, demanding to know what was going on.

"It's fine," I assured him. "These fine men were just helping me up after I tripped."

The sarcasm in my voice was unmistakable.

We were brought back to our room without further incident, and the bags were removed from our heads.

My pages on the table had been moved while we were gone. Someone had looked through them.

Did they think I was hiding something from them?

How stupid. Even if I was, I wouldn't leave it lying around for them to find so easily.

Our captors left, and the door was locked behind them. The moment we were alone, Kayden immediately grabbed my shoulders and spun me to face him, his face twisted in worry.

"Are you okay? I heard you fall. Did they hurt you?"

"I'm fine," I insisted again. When we'd first been locked in here, I'd checked every inch of the room for hidden cameras or microphones. By now, I was certain that they weren't watching us or listening in, so I confidently held up my hand and unclenched my fist.

The nail sat on my palm.

"I'm going to get us out of here."

***

After our meeting with Chester Grieve, I was more unsettled than before.

The man wanted something out of us, out of me specifically, more than just the journal. He was looking for an answer to a question I couldn't even fathom.

I was left even more determined not to give the man what he wanted. At the moment, it was a moot point as I hadn't cracked the journal yet, but even when I did, I couldn't give it to him.

Our only hope would be to escape before I finished the journal.

After our meeting, other members of the cult checked on us more frequently than before. At least once an hour during the day someone would come by looking for an update on what progress I'd made. Each time, I had to have something to show them, or they threatened to move Kayden to a separate room.

Because of this, I had to keep working on the journal. So, I handed the nail over to Kayden to take care of.

While I was busy writing out codes, Kayden sat on the floor, painstakingly rubbing the nail against the concrete wall and slowly filing it down into a thin point. Old locks were bulkier than new ones, and had bigger keyholes, so it was my hope that the nail could be filed down into something that could be used to pick the lock.

That was step one of our escape plans. After that, I still wasn't sure what to do, but it was a start.

A knock came at the door. Kayden quickly hid the half-filed nail up his sleeve. A knock meant it was probably Robyn bringing our next meal, but we couldn't be too careful.

I called out for the boy to enter.

When he opened the door, I caught a glimpse up the stairs beyond where I could just see several armed men standing guard.

My view of our guards only lasted a moment before the door shut behind the boy and we were once more cut off.

"How are you doing, Robyn?" Kayden asked as the boy set his laden tray down on the table. His voice sounded concerned.

Robyn muttered a quiet "Fine" as he started setting out the different dishes.

I could see why Kayden sounded so

concerned. Robyn's complexion was paler than normal, and there were heavy circles under his eyes. His hands shook, causing him to fumble and drop one of the bowls.

I managed to catch it, grateful for the lid on the bowl, or else its contents would have ended up on the floor.

"Whoa, Robyn, sit down," Kayden insisted, pulling out a chair for the boy.

It took very little coaxing before the boy practically collapsed into the offered chair and hung his head in his hands.

"I shouldn't stay here," he spoke straight at the floor. "They'll be suspicious if I take too long."

Kayden knelt beside the boy's chair, stroking a soothing hand over his back. "Okay. Just take a moment to breathe and then you can go. What's wrong? Is there anything we can do?"

It was a meaningless offer. We could barely take care of ourselves let alone do anything to help the boy, but Kayden's concern seemed to calm the boy down, nonetheless.

The young man sucked in a deep breath; some of the color returned to his skin and he sat up straight.

"Are you trying to escape from here?"

Kayden and I shared an equally baffled look.

"Um," Kayden stumbled over his words. "That's not..."

Robyn interrupted, his words gaining speed as he started to ramble. "Everyone says that you're some kind of expert soldier, and that you must have some plan to try and escape. That's why we must be careful with you."

At this, Kayden was completely speechless, but before I could try to respond, Robyn whispered one last sentence.

"I hope they're right."

His words were spoken under his breath, as if he was afraid to even let them touch the air.

Bracing myself for what I was about to hear—because I could tell from Robyn's tone that it wouldn't be good—I knelt beside the boy as well and asked him to explain.

The story came rushing out of him in one tangled mess of whispered words.

He'd been in charge of taking care of his sister, Mavis, since their parents died. Recently, he'd overheard some of the elders of their community making plans for who Mavis should marry.

The girl was only six.

Apparently, *The Tamed Souls* had been losing people over the years, and they were desperate to increase their numbers. So, they were encouraging their members to marry earlier and earlier.

Ordinarily, a child's parents would have the final say in their marriage, but with no living parents, Mavis and Robyn were helpless against the desires of the adults around them.

The moment Mavis was physically developed enough to bear children, she'd be married off, and there was no telling how old her husband would be.

By the end of his explanation, Robyn was clinging to my arm, tugging at me as he begged.

"Please, if you escape from here, please take my sister with you. I can't watch this happen to her. I'll do anything."

Comforting children was never one of my strong suits. I awkwardly patted the boy on the head, hoping it would soothe him at least a little bit, as I shared another look with Kayden.

Even without exchanging a word, we were both in agreement.

"I'll do you one better," I said to the boy. "You and your sister can both come with us. But I'll need something from you first."

Robyn sniffed and wiped away tears

that hadn't fallen yet, looking up at me with a fearful hope in his eyes. "Anything."

"First, I need a watch or something that will keep track of time. We can't even tell if it's day or night in here."

Robyn instantly started nodding, even before I'd finished speaking.

I held up a hand to get his attention again.

"And second... what can you tell me about those guards by the door?"

***

Robyn was right. The guards were suspicious after he took longer to drop off our meal than normal. Now the guards were on high alert, so we wouldn't be able to act right away. We'd have to wait a couple days until that suspicion calmed down again.

This gave us plenty of time to plan.

Robyn was careful to never loiter in

our room again. He delivered the information we needed a few sentences at a time whenever he dropped off a meal.

With each new delivery, a picture began to form in my mind. Many guards gathered around when our door was opened, but other than that, there was usually only one person standing by the entrance to the building. Furthermore, there was a group of guardsmen that patrolled the village at night. They technically covered the entire perimeter of the area, but they didn't pay as much attention to the north side of the village where most of the buildings were empty.

"Why are you still working on that?" Kayden asked as he continued to file down the nail. It was mostly done, and he just needed to refine the point of the tip into the correct shape.

I looked down at the papers spread out before me where I was still working on cracking the code of the journal. "If my work pace suddenly slows down, they'll get suspicious. Plus, I can probably buy us some time by handing over part of the journal."

The relentless sound of iron scrapping against concrete stopped when Kayden set down the nail and came over to look at my work.

"So, you figured it out?"

I held up one of the pages that held legible words. "Partially. It looks like Lisianthus used several different codes in her journal. I've managed to figure out one of them. I'm going to make sure there isn't any dangerous information in the journal, but assuming it's harmless, I can hand over this part to keep our captors off our backs for a while."

After pressing a kiss to my temple, Kayden stored the nail up his sleeve and then threw himself down on the mattress.

"What information could the journal hold that would be dangerous for us?"

CREED

I tapped my pen against the table. When my mind was too busy, I often calmed myself down by absently writing or doodling. So often, I'd wished for pen and paper when my stress was high and there was nothing to write with.

Now, I had too much to write, and I needed a distraction from my usual distraction.

"Dangerous may not be the right word," I said as I drew a trail of dots along the edge of one page. "But our captors are looking for something in this journal. Once they get what they're looking for, they have no reason to keep us around. I want to make sure I don't accidentally hand over their answer too early."

The code that Lisianthus used on her journal was a simple one. What made it so hard to decipher was the fact that she used multiple layers of simple code.

A single snowflake was light, but an avalanche could kill a man. In the same way, many simple codes overlapping each other made for a very complicated puzzle to figure out.

She'd also changed the code system she'd used for different parts of the journal. For now, I'd only figured out the first part.

The beginning of the journal talked about the sister's initial escape from *The Tamed Souls*, and how they'd pulled it off.

It hadn't been as simple as just walking out the door one day. They had spent weeks planning, secretly hording supplies and money. However, the biggest obstacle had been the cult founder, their shared husband. He was a vigilant man and kept close tabs on his wives.

Either he was a naturally suspicious man, or he already knew that they hated being married to him and wanted to escape.

I had to take a break after translating how the sisters would take turns going to him at night to keep him distracted so that the remaining two could keep safely working on their escape plan. There were no specific details given, but the meaning was still clear. I practically felt like I was right alongside the sisters when Lisianthus talked about the dread she felt when her night came. Yet, she faced it without complaint since the one thing she dreaded more than her husband, was forcing her sisters to bear her share of the burden.

I could relate.

Not the part about having to appease an unwanted husband, but the need to keep moving forward even when you wanted to give up, just so that you didn't burden those you cared about.

How many times had I faced similar situations with Magnus and Brody?

How many times had I kept fighting, not because I cared about my own life, but because I feared that if I died there would be no one to watch their backs.

It was what had helped me survive when I was a prisoner of war, and it was what would help me survive now.

Luckily Lisianthus didn't spend too much time detailing how the sisters planed for their escape, but the next part of the journal was even more shocking.

"Coffee beans?" Kayden gasped in surprise when I told him.

"That's what it says." I pointed to the paragraph I'd just translated. "Apparently, the key to their escape was coffee beans. They came up with a plan to drug their husband, along with all the most important people in the cult, during a monthly meeting that the founder always held."

By this point, Kayden and I were sitting together on the bed as we looked over the part of the journal I'd translated. It almost felt like I was reading a bedtime story, except the story wasn't so innocent and our situation was much more dire.

"Drugged them?" Kayden asked, tracing his fingers over the words I'd written. "That was ballsy of them. If they were so heavily monitored, how'd they pull it off?"

"By going right to the source. Everything that came in or out of their home was scrutinized. There was no way for them to add anything extra to the founder's food, so they altered the food itself. Rose had an extraordinary green thumb and grew a lot of their food in her own garden. So, she bred a new type of coffee bean that acted as a natural sedative. They gave it to the founder and all the guests at the meeting. No one suspected a thing since it came from the founder's own garden, and they knew nothing extra had been added to the coffee. The natural sedative had a delayed effect, so that night all the important people in the cult went to sleep and didn't wake up for twenty-four hours, giving the sisters plenty of time to make their escape without being followed."

I barely paid attention to what I was saying, more focused on the feeling of Kayden pressed warmly against my side.

The bed was barely big enough for one of us, let alone both. In order to keep from falling off, Kayden had to press himself as close to my side as possible, using my shoulder as his pillow and throwing one arm across my waist like a seatbelt.

In a different setting, I would have enjoyed it.

"That explains the coffee beans in the locket."

I was so lost in thought, admiring the feel of Kayden pressed against me, that I almost missed what he said.

"What do you mean?"

He had to turn himself awkwardly to look up at me and still stay on the mattress.

"In Rose's locket, along with the map to the hidden mausoleum, there were also coffee beans. This explains it. The sisters held onto the beans as their literal smoking gun. It was proof of how they'd escaped. Also, probably a safety measure, in case they ever needed to escape again."

It was a sensible conclusion. I was just surprised that I hadn't thought of it first. I hadn't been there when the others discovered the secret of Rose's locket, so it had slipped my mind. I hadn't even realized Kayden knew about the locket at all.

"Magnus and Brody told you about the locket?"

Kayden just shrugged. "I didn't have much to do while you were getting ready for our trip, so I asked your friends about what happened. They gave me a summary of everything. I've got a good memory for detail, otherwise I'd never be able to remember enough about my trips to write about them."

His whole body stiffened up and his eyes grew wide before he suddenly sat upright on the very edge of the bed.

"Oh, fuck!"

"What's wrong?" I asked, alarmed, as I also sat up.

"I'm not going to be able to write about any of this. What the hell am I going to give to my editor?"

Sighing, I wrapped my arms around him. "How about we focus on staying alive first. Then we can worry about your editor."

He ran both hands through his brown hair, nearly pulling it out by the roots. "No, you don't understand. My editor's a total hard-ass. She'll kill me if I don't have a new article by the deadline. Seriously, I may as well just let the cult kill me. They'll probably be more merciful."

Trying not to roll my eyes at his dramatics, I pulled Kayden back down onto the bed and found much more pleasant ways to distract him.

***

Three days after our last meeting with Chester Grieve, we were finally ready to make our escape. The plans were in place. All we needed was the right opportunity.

Waiting for nightfall was aggravating. I watched the seconds tick by on the watch that Robyn had brought us, trying to will time to go faster.

The boy was smarter than he gave himself credit for. I'd only asked him to bring us a watch or clock of some sort since I didn't know what he'd be able to get his hands on. He'd had the foresight to bring us a digital watch instead of an analog one, so that it wouldn't make any ticking noises that could be discovered. Plus, the glowing numbers were easier to see in the dark.

The boy would do well for himself, if we

could get him away from these extremists.

Finally, after hours of excruciating waiting, it was time to act.

Kayden handed me the nail he'd so tirelessly filed into shape. "Let's see if this works."

Ideally, I would have preferred two tools to pick the lock, but we hadn't been lucky enough to come across any other pieces of suitable metal.

One would have to do.

The lock on the door was old but well maintained, with no signs of rust or any damage. Its keyhole was larger than modern locks, and the filed down nail easily slipped inside.

Several tense moments passed as I navigated the inside of the lock entirely by feel, coaxing the tumblers into place one by one.

The lock clicked when the last tumbler fell.

Kayden and I stood in silence, barely

daring to breath as we waited to see if anyone had heard us. I pressed my ear to the thick wood of the door but couldn't hear anything.

Now for the hard part.

Without a second lock pick, I'd have to use the nail to turn the lock while keeping all the tumblers in place. I'd instructed Kayden to file the nail down into a flat pointed shape, similar to a key, but it was a fine line. The pick needed to be thin enough to manipulate the tumblers, but sturdy enough to turn the lock on its own. There was no way to test it beforehand.

If the nail snapped off in the lock, then this whole escape plan was over before it even started.

Holding my breath, I turned the lock.

The door swung open.

Kayden and I stared into the open doorway at the staircase that would lead us to freedom.

I grabbed his hand.

"Let's go," I said, making sure to whisper.

Rather than respond, Kayden just nodded and gripped my hand back in a tight grip.

He didn't let go, even as we ascended the stairs.

CHAPTER EIGHT

Kayden

THE STAIRCASE WASN'T as tall as I thought. Every time I'd been brought up and down that staircase while blinded with a bag over my head, it had felt like we were deep underground.

Now that I could see, it turned out it was only a single flight of stairs. Just sixteen steps stood between us and the outside.

Well, sixteen steps and a guard.

Creed tapped my chest and pushed me

against the wall. "Wait here."

I stayed exactly where he left me, listening in the dark as he vanished from sight around the corner. A moment later there was a small gasp, and then a heavy thud.

"Creed?" I called out, torn between avoiding detection and needing to know that he was all right.

My one-word question earned an immediate response, and Creed popped his head back around the corner.

"It's all right. Come here and help me with this."

Looking around the corner for myself, I found him standing there holding the unconscious body of the guard up by its arms. Under Creed's instruction, I grabbed the guard's feet, and together we dragged the man back down the stairs to our makeshift prison and locked him inside.

"Hopefully, I've timed this right," Creed

said once we'd finished. "They'll notice something is wrong as soon as the guards change shifts, but based on the schedule Robyn told me, that shouldn't be for a few hours. It's not as much time as I'd like, but it should be enough for us to make our getaway."

"Then let's get moving."

Grabbing onto Creed's hand again, mostly for my own assurance that I wouldn't lose him in the dark, we headed outside.

The village wasn't just old-fashioned in its customs, it was also old-fashioned in its technology. There were very few outdoor lights, and the few that did exist were only used to illuminate the main path.

There was also very little natural light. Luck was on our side, and the moon was a mere sliver in the sky, barely any better than a new moon. This made the night even darker than usual. I could barely see my hand in front of my own face. So long as we avoided the center of the village, we could easily go unnoticed.

It was also eerily quiet. Even my own breathing felt like it echoed. I stepped as carefully as I could and leaned in to whisper directly into Creed's ear whenever I had to speak.

"Where are we meeting Robyn?"

"He said to meet him at the abandoned schoolhouse. It's near the edge of the village, but apparently, it's been shut down for a while. Not enough kids to make it worthwhile."

It was a comprehensive answer, but it didn't really help me. I had no idea where the schoolhouse was located, or even which direction to go to get to the outer edge of the village. I was glad Creed seemed to know where he was going, because if I was left to navigate on my own, I'd probably have stumbled my way right into Chester Grieve's bedroom.

CREED

Give me proper roads and street signs and I could navigate my way across any unfamiliar city. However, in places like this, where none of the streets had names and everything was described with a mere cardinal direction, I was completely lost.

It was only going to get worse when we left the village behind and headed out into the forest.

With this in mind, I clung tighter to Creed's hand.

The old schoolhouse looked like something out of a picture book. It was a single room building that had once been painted red, though most of the paint was flaking off now, and even had a little steeple with a bell on top. I could easily imagine the idyllic setting it had once created, and almost understood how people were originally sucked into the cult.

Now, however, the building just looked sad.

Robyn waited for us just inside the schoolhouse door, angled so that he could see out without anyone else seeing him.

"You made it out," he greeted us when we arrived. There were too many lines on this child's face. He looked stressed beyond his years, but some of those worry lines flattened out when he saw us.

His posture was also unnaturally hunched. At first, I thought this was also a result of the stress he was under, until we got closer, and I saw that he was carrying his sister on his back.

Mavis was small, even for a six-year-old, but Robyn was only twelve and his sister was half his size. There was also a large backpack sitting at his feet, completely stuffed to the brim. The bag was nearly the same size as his sister, and I had no idea how he'd managed to carry both out here.

Creed knelt beside the kids and placed his hand on the girl's forehead. "Is she still not feeling well?"

Mavis didn't even stir under Creed's touch, and Robyn shook his head sadly.

"It's just a cold. She'll be fine."

Worry gripped my heart. Robyn had told us about his sister's illness before, but I hadn't considered what that would mean for us. We were headed out into the wilderness with little more than the clothes on our backs. Even a simple cold could be dangerous for a child in that kind of environment.

"We'll have to carry the little one," Creed said, automatically reaching for the girl. Robyn was understandably hesitant to hand over his sister, but Creed remained patient despite our tight time limit. "I promise I'm not going to run off with her. We have a long distance to travel. You won't be able to carry her that far, and you're no help to her if you wear yourself out trying."

Biting his lip with indecision, Robyn

eventually nodded and transferred his sister onto Creed's back. Then he tried to pick up the backpack, but I beat him to it and grabbed it for myself.

"Don't worry about this. Just focus on yourself."

Robyn eyed me with suspicion. "Are you sure? It's heavy."

I withheld my urge to laugh through the insult. Creed and I were almost the same size, but his bulk mostly came from muscle that had been honed over decades of training. My size clearly came from a life of too much fine dining mixed with hours sitting at a desk.

"I'll manage," I assured him as I slung the bag onto my back. Oddly enough, although the bag was large, it wasn't as heavy as the pack I'd been carrying for our original hiking trip. Even over just a couple of days Creed had already helped whip me into better shape.

Once everything was settled, Robyn

showed us to the tall fence surrounding the entire village. It was at least eight feet high, made of solid wood, and only had a few entry and exit points.

The more I saw of this village, the more it seemed like a prison disguised as a home. This was not a place meant for people to live freely.

"Over here," Robyn said, waving us toward one particular board in the fence. "This board broke during a storm a few months ago, and no one bothered to fix it. I dug out under it as much as I could."

In the dark it was hard to tell, but on closer inspection I could see where Robyn had excavated some of the dirt out from under the fence. Based on the marks in the ground, he seemed to have done it by hand. It wasn't very deep, but once the loose board was moved out of the way, there was a decent size gap left.

Decent sized for a child, at least. Creed and I were another matter.

"Are we going to fit through there?" I whispered to Creed.

"Only one way to find out," he replied, equally quiet.

Robyn went first, easily shimmying under the fence. His sister was then passed through next. We had to wake the poor girl up so she could crawl on her own. Blearily eyes looked around, clearly confused, but she was drawn to the sound of her brother's voice on the other side of the fence and followed it without question, crawling on her hands and knees in the dirt.

Then only Creed and I remained.

We shared a look, and Creed shrugged. "Here goes nothing."

He had to lie flat in the dirt to even have a chance of fitting through the gap. He couldn't even prop himself up on his elbows to army crawl. Instead, he had to reach forward and drag himself purely by his arms like the world's most uncoordinated snake. His shoulders could only fit through one at a time, and his feet kicked in the dirt for more traction to help push himself forward, but once the majority of his chest was through the fence, the rest of him followed pretty easily.

Once he was free, I shoved the backpack through the hole after him. Then I was the last one still trapped on this side of the fence.

Taking a deep breath, I lowered myself down onto the ground. Once I was face to face with the opening, it looked even smaller than I thought. It was a miracle Creed had even fit, and I could see fibers from his shirt stuck to the wood planks where he'd scraped along the fence.

Creed's face appeared on the other side of the hole, turned at an odd angle where he was crouching in order to see me.

"It's all right. Just go slow. And if you get stuck, don't panic. Tensing up will only made it harder to fit through."

I followed Creed's technique, keeping the rest of my body flat and relaxed, and gripping onto either side of the hole in order to pull myself with just my arms. I wasn't as strong as him. Dragging my entire weight left my arms trembling from the strain.

My head and shoulders fit through easier than Creed's had, and for a moment I had hope that everything would go smoothly.

Then, when the side planks of the fence touched my stomach, I came to a sudden stop.

"Fuck," I sighed under my breath and let my forehead fall to the dirt.

It was as I'd feared.

Creed and I were both large men, but Creed's broadest point was his shoulders, which could be maneuvered to fit through one at a time.

My broadest point was my stomach,

which couldn't be manipulated nearly as well.

"It's okay," Creed said above my head. "Just stay relaxed and give me your hands."

I stuck out my arms for Creed to grab, and he tried to pull me through from his side of the fence, but I wouldn't budge.

I was thoroughly stuck in the fence.

Lying face down in the dirt, I started to laugh.

"You know, I think I've seen porn that started this way."

I couldn't see Creed's face from my position, but I could feel his confusion radiating above me.

Right. The man had spent his life stuck deep in the closet. He'd probably never even watched porn before.

After a moment of consideration, Creed prodded at the parts of my midsection that he could reach. "Are you trying to suck in your stomach?"

"Yes, of course, but it's clearly not enough."

"Stop doing that. Just let everything relax?"

I craned my head as best I could to look at him, raising one eyebrow in silent doubt.

"Trust me," he insisted. "I know it sounds counterintuitive, but by holding in your stomach you're tensing up everything else, and tense muscles aren't as malleable as soft ones."

There wasn't much choice but to trust him. It took a moment for me to relax and let every muscle in my body go slack. I felt my stomach press more firmly against the ground and the sides of the fence and couldn't help doubting Creed's assessment.

Creed picked up my hands again. "Ready? Before I pull, exhale all the air from your lungs then hold your breath. It'll help."

I did as he said, and when my lungs were as empty as possible, I nodded.

He pulled.

The planks of the fence dug painfully into my flesh, and I was probably going to have some deep scrapes after this, but surprisingly, I started to slide forward inch by inch.

My stomach was almost through the fence, when I was abruptly jerked back to a stop.

"What now?" I gasped. The wooden planks squeezing me from either side was making it very hard to breath, and I was starting to feel dizzy from the limited air.

Creed dropped my hands to prod around at my waist again.

"Take off your pants."

My eyes nearly bugged out of my head. "What?"

"Your pants are caught on the fence. Probably because you came to a stop. I can't reach the other side of the fence to un-snag them, so try to at least unbutton them."

I sighed again. "I have definitely seen porn that started this way."

Maybe making sexual jokes in the presence of children wasn't a great thing to do but damn it all, I needed something to help me keep calm, and inappropriate humor was the only tool I had to rely on in that moment.

It took some wiggling, but I managed to get a hand under myself and undo the button and zipper of my pants. Then Creed dragged me by my arms once again, and this time I slid right out of my pants and the rest of the way through the fence.

I was half naked, dirty, and covered in bloody scratches, but I was free.

"That's it," I muttered as I retrieved my pants from the other side of the fence and started putting them back on. "After this, I'm going on a diet."

Creed grabbed me and spun me around to face him with an alarmed look on his face.

"Don't you dare."

His gaze flickered down over my body, covetous and hungry in a way that I'd never been looked at before.

It was reassuring to know that he enjoyed my figure just the way it was, and I patted his arm in a show of comfort.

"Don't worry. I've said the same thing many times before and it's never happened."

Creed's eyes narrowed as he continued to stare at me, like he thought I would suddenly start losing weight right in front of him.

"Good," he eventually declared, then turned around to take Mavis back from Robyn so we could continue our escape.

I just shook my head, picked up the backpack, and followed him.

Navigating our way through the forest

in the dark was nothing like the hike Creed had taken me on earlier. I'd thought the previous hike was hard, but it was practically a stroll through the park compared to this. We had a flashlight, but Creed claimed that waving a light around in the middle of the night would make us easier to find, so we stumbled our way through the dark. There wasn't a path, not even a natural deer trail that we could follow, so we were forced to stomp our way directly through the underbrush while trying to leave as little evidence of our passing as possible.

I had no idea how Creed did it. The man must secretly be part cat, because despite his size, he barely left any footprints, and easily navigated between the trees as if it were broad daylight. He did all this while also carrying a mostly unconscious child and didn't even look like he was breaking a sweat.

In contrast, I nearly smacked my face

directly into a tree trunk three times in the first hour.

"Do you even know where we're going, or are we just wandering around blindly?" I asked when we stopped to catch our breath for a moment.

I had no illusion that the break was mostly for Robyn's sake. If it had just been the two of us, Creed would have insisted we keep going. In bed, I enjoyed that kind of confident control, but in this case, it was just annoying.

I couldn't even get mad at him for it. Creed's unrelenting spirit was the thing most likely to help us survive.

"I know where we're going," he assured me as he handed me one of the water bottles from the bag that Robyn had supplied.

The boy had been smart enough to pack plenty of essentials. We had enough food and water for a few days so long as we used it sparingly.

I only took a brief sip of water, saving as much of it as I could.

"How can you possibly know where we're going? We're out in the middle of nowhere."

Rather than answer me with words, Creed merely pointed toward the sky.

I looked up, seeing the cloudless night sky above us dotted with thousands of stars.

Of course, the man could navigate purely by the sight of the stars.

Why was I even surprised?

That kind of competency was hot, don't get me wrong, but still...

What the hell?

Why would he even know that kind of stuff?

Surely the military had more sophisticated navigational technology.

"We escaped on the north side of the village," Creed explained. "We'll head east for a bit to ensure we give the area a wide berth, and then we'll head south. If we are where I think we are, there should be a town just a few days hike from here."

He was already starting to pack up again, ready to continue our journey.

I groaned but hoisted myself off of the tree I was leaning against.

"Isn't there a road or something we can follow? We were brought there in a van. That means there is some way to travel to and from the village."

Creed handed me the bag before picking up Mavis again and carefully positioning her on his back.

"The road is the first place they'll look for us. If we want to avoid getting caught, we have to stay as far from the road as possible."

The bag may not have been as heavy as the one I was carrying when we started our little hiking trip, but it still weighed on me as I hoisted it onto my shoulder. I groaned as the straps settled into place and prepared myself to continue the difficult journey.

"I can take that," Robyn offered, reaching for the bag.

Summoning up more energy, I forced my face into a smile that I hoped looked genuine.

"Don't worry. I've got it. This isn't my first time hiking across a mountain."

Technically, it was my second time, but the boy didn't need to know that.

We kept going, slowly but steadily. The sounds of the night followed us everywhere, leaving the hair on the back of my neck in a permanently upright position. It felt like we were constantly being watched, and with every unidentifiable noise my imagination kept flipping between the cult we were running from and the natural dangers of the forest.

I wasn't sure which was worse.

After another hour of hiking, we came

upon a small river. I wasn't sure what the difference between a river and a stream was, but the water here was deep enough and moving fast enough that calling it a river seemed appropriate.

Creed showed no sign of surprise when we reached the river, so I assumed he somehow knew it was there. He checked the direction the river, looking at the sky a few times to cross-reference whatever information was in his head, before declaring "This is a good spot."

Sensing that we were about to stop for a while, I set the bag down. "A good spot for what?"

Creed also laid Mavis on a large flat rock.

"To throw them off our trail. I don't know if they have any scent hounds, or expert trackers, but just in case, we should leave a false trail. Give me your shoes."

Assuming that Creed had a plan,

because at this point it was safe to assume he always had a plan, Robyn and I took off our shoes and handed them over without question. We each stood on a rock to keep our socks out of the dirt and watched as Creed walked along the riverbank, stopping occasionally to press our shoes into the soft mud of the riverbank and leave false tracks to make it look like three people were walking side by side.

He continued until he reached a rockier area where our shoes wouldn't leave any obvious tracks, then he walked backward along his own footprints until he returned to us.

"Here, put these back on and let's keep going. It'll be daylight soon enough, and we need to find shelter before then."

"Since you laid the false trail going downstream, I assume we're not going that way," I said as I laced up my boots. "So where are we going?"

CREED

Creed pointed across the river. "We'll cross here. The water will help wash away our scent, and the opposite bank has plenty of large rocks we can climb out on without leaving obvious footprints.

The moment I stepped into the water, I shivered. It was colder than I expected for the middle of summer. According to Creed, the rivers this far into the mountain probably came from the snow melting off their peaks, but I still hadn't expected it to be quite so cold.

Robyn yelped the moment he stepped foot into the water, and quickly covered his hands over his mouth to stifle the noise. He'd accidentally stepped into the deeper area, and the water reached halfway up his thigh.

I held onto him as we waded through the river, making sure he didn't get swept away. The water wasn't too deep, only coming up to about my waist at its deepest point, but the current was strong, and it could be dangerous if it took our feet out from under us.

We stepped carefully over the loose rocks and slimy plants until we reached the opposite riverbank. Once out of the river, the night air hit my wet skin like someone had dumped ice inside my clothing. I shivered strong enough to make my teeth chatter and hugged my arms close to my chest.

"How much... farther?" I asked, trying not to bite my own tongue when I talked.

Creed looked at Robyn and I shivering with a sympathetic expression. He'd kept Mavis out of the water, so she was dry, and although he was also wet, he showed no signs that he even noticed the cold.

"Not much farther. We just need to get far enough away from the river so that if they aren't fooled by the false trail, then they still won't easily find us."

Apparently, to Creed "not much farther" meant another two hours of hiking. Based on the watch strapped to his wrist, it was just past five in the morning when we saw the first signs of daylight in the sky. We'd escaped some time around one in the morning, so we'd only been hiking for about four hours, yet it felt like we'd been walking for days.

"Here," Creed finally announced, pointing to a patch of forest that looked no different than anywhere else.

I stood there, doubled over with my hands on my knees as I tried to catch my breath.

"Here, what?"

Creed pulled back a bush to reveal a small opening in the rocks that I hadn't even noticed.

"We'll take shelter here for the day and continue our journey once night falls. This should be safe enough."

The entrance of the cave wasn't very big, bit inside it was more spacious than I expected. Part of it must have extended underground. I'd just been held in an underground room for days, so the thought of returning underground wasn't very appealing, but I had to admit it was a great choice for shelter. The ground was dry and comfortable, and the entrance was nearly invisible from the outside.

I threw the bag off my back and collapsed onto the earthen floor. "How did you know this was here? I didn't even see it when we were standing right next to it."

Creed lay Mavis down on the ground farther back in the cave and encouraged Robyn to remove his damp clothes so they could dry properly.

"I figured there had to be a cave of some sort around here based on what the Milford sisters described."

To my shock, he pulled out several pages of the translated journal that he'd made. I hadn't realized he'd brought any of it with him, but he'd apparently stuffed as many as he could inside his pockets.

"Lisianthus gave a detailed description of their escape and their journey through the mountains. The landscape has changed over the last hundred and twenty-five years, but it's still similar enough for her descriptions to be useful. I just wish I'd been able to translate more of it before we left. There might be more information in the journal about this mountain that we could use."

"I can help with that," Robyn piped up from the back of the cave.

He left his sister's side to root through the pockets of the supply bag. There hadn't been time for either Creed or I to thoroughly inspect the bag, so we didn't know what exactly it held other than the basics.

To both of our shock, after a moment of searching, Robyn held up a very familiar journal.

Creed accepted the offered journal, turning it over in his hands like he feared it would suddenly turn to dust. "You took this?"

Robyn dug the toes of one bare foot into the dirt, sheepishly not looking at any of us. He had stripped down to us underwear in order to lay his wet clothes out to dry, leaving his embarrassed blush on full display as it spread past his face and down onto his chest.

"Yeah. I just... everyone was so obsessed with the thing, so I figured it had to be important, right? If it's important, then it can probably help us. Nobody in the community really pays attention to me, so I can come and go from most places in the village without notice."

With careful fingers, Creed flipped through the pages. Until now, he'd been working entirely from pictures of the journal, and never actually seen the real thing. It was a sturdy leather book with a particularly thick binding. Whoever made it, whether it was one of the Milford sisters or someone else, had ensured that the journal was strong enough to last through the ages.

"Was that all right?" Robyn asked, still looking very self-conscious. "I know stealing is wrong, but kidnapping is worse, isn't it? Is it okay to do something wrong if it's to fix a bigger wrong?"

Creed closed the journal with a snap, and carefully set it aside on a rock so it stayed well out of the dirt.

"It's definitely okay. Plus, this journal was stolen to begin with. You're just returning it to its rightful owners."

He led Robyn back to his sister before the boy could bring up any more questions of reality. The last thing we needed was Robyn having a crisis of conscience on our hands on top of everything else. To keep the boy distracted, Creed insisted that he wake up his sister and try to get her to eat and drink something. She was sick and needed to keep her strength up, but she probably wouldn't appreciate being hounded by two strange men she didn't know.

Robyn instantly agreed, and once he was fully engaged with his sister, Creed returned to the front of the cave.

"That boy doesn't realize what he's done," he said as he sat down next to me. "That journal will be a great bargaining chip with the cult, but it'll also make them a thousand times more determined to find us. On our own, they might have been willing to let us go. But with the journal... well, we've already seen the lengths they're willing to go to."

I knelt in the dirt near the cave entrance, taking off my clothing one piece at a time and spreading it out in a patch of morning sunlight. My skin was still damp and covered in goosebumps, but I no longer felt quite as uncomfortable once my wet clothing was removed.

"We'll survive," I said, trying to sound more certain than I felt. "We just need to get to a town and then call your friends for help, right? Easy. We'll be safely out of here before those insane cultists even come close to finding us."

With my clothing taken care of, I sat down beside Creed and cuddled up to him for warmth.

"You know, watching you be a one-man A-Team has been pretty hot."

The smirk that Creed gave me was unfairly attractive. "Really?"

"Oh yeah." I trailed a discrete hand up his thigh. "If we were alone in this cave right now, I'd definitely be jumping you."

I sighed, letting him feel exactly how disappointed I was.

"I guess I'll just have to wait until later. So, for now, you better hold me. I'm wet and cold, and it's all your fault."

Creed didn't utter a word of protest as

he complied with my request.

CHAPTER NINE

Creed

EVEN IN SUMMER, days in the mountains were cold. The bag of supplies Robyn had brought was invaluable; we weren't in danger of going hungry for the next few days, but we still had no tent. Even Kayden and I would find it difficult to rough it in the forest. For the children, especially Mavis, who still suffered from a severe cold, it could be fatal.

We needed to make sure we had proper shelter to sleep, if nothing else.

That first day in the cave, while our wet clothes dried in a patch of sunlight near the fire, I pulled out Lisianthus's journal. Without paper or pen to write with, translating the code was more difficult, but not impossible. It was slow going, but word by word, I managed to piece together what the next few pages said.

Lisianthus Milford—I would not call her Grieve since that wasn't the name she had chosen—had meticulously planned out their escape route long before they left the cult and she'd written all of it down, explaining in detail where their plans worked, and where the natural landscape caused them to deviate.

It was coming in handy now. Although not as good as an actual map, it was the next best thing, and I was able to come up with a general plan for our route through the woods.

"Still focused on that journal?" Kayden

asked when he sat down next to me. He'd been helping to take care of the kids, making sure they ate.

A pair of soft snores from the back of the next cave we'd taken shelter in told me that they were asleep, kept warm by the fire and the majority of our blankets and dry clothing.

Even as Kayden settled in next to me, the heat of his body chasing away the coolness of the stone I was leaning against. I didn't dare look at him directly. Most of his clothing was again drying by the fire, leaving him in just a pair of boxers.

A cave in the middle of the wilderness, taking shelter with two children, was no place for me to be getting excited, but I couldn't help my body's reaction to the sight of him.

Just to be safe, I kept my eyes firmly glued on the words and rough maps that I'd scratched into the dirt.

"If my remembered map is correct, and the information in Lisianthus's journal is mostly accurate, then we should be able to reach a town, Whimborne, in about two days."

Kayden studied what I'd drawn out in the dirt, careful not to touch anything.

"So, you know where we are?"

I nodded. "Yes. Since the Milford sisters managed to travel there on foot, I knew it was doable, but there was never an accurate account of how long it took them. Luckily, we aren't as far from Emberwood as I feared."

"So, we get to Whimborne. Then what?"

"Then we find the nearest phone and call for help. Magnus and Brody could probably drive out to us in a few hours."

"Call your friends?" Kayden gave me a strange look. "Is that really what we should do first? What about the police? We were kidnapped. That's... highly illegal. Surely, contacting the police should be our first priority."

Before he'd even finished speaking, I was already shaking my head. Despite being a world traveler, it was easy to forget how innocent Kayden actually was.

"In small towns out in rural areas like this, everyone knows everyone. There're probably at least a few members of the Tamed Souls on the local police force. No. It's too much of a risk. If we call Brody and Magnus, then at least we know help is on the way. They can decide how much law enforcement needs to be involved."

Hunkering down more next to me, Kayden wrapped himself tighter in the one blanket he'd kept for himself. It seemed to be a child's blanket, and barely fit around him as he laid his head on my shoulder.

"You know more about this stuff, so I'll have to take your word for it."

I ran a hand through his hair, already

feeling his muscles relaxing as he began drifting off to sleep.

"Don't worry. I promise, I'll get us through this."

Kayden mumbled something that was probably meant to be an agreement, but he drifted off mid-sentence, and his words turned in a subtle snoring.

Chuckling to myself, I turned my attention back to the journal.

Translating the code without paper and pen to write with was a lot harder. I could scratch out some words in the dirt, but a lot of the conversion had to be done in my head, and there was no way to permanently record anything that I did manage to figure out.

Because of this, when the next word I translated from the journal made no sense, I assumed I'd just messed up somewhere.

I worked through the code again, making sure to carve out everything in the dirt to ensure its accuracy.

The word remained the same.

"Wait." I glared down at the page, certain that I must have misunderstood something. "That can't be right, can it?"

I moved on to the rest of the sentence, hoping that maybe some context would give me a better understanding of what the journal was talking about.

It did. After just a few more sentences of translation, I fully understood what the journal was talking about; I just didn't understand why Lisianthus had changed from her detailed record of their escape, to such a... seemingly random topic.

I couldn't go to sleep, since someone had to keep a look out in case our pursuers caught up with us. Kayden had agreed to switch off with me halfway through the night so I could also get some sleep, but that still left me with many hours where I had nothing to do but obsess over Lisianthus's writing.

And the story contained within her journal had just taken an interesting twist.

***

Our luck held out for the next few days. There were no signs of our pursuers so we'd moved to traveling during the day instead of at night. The weather remained calm, without a hint of rain or other conditions that could slow us down. Plus, Mavis's cold finally broke. We still had to carry her. She wasn't back to full health yet, and even if she was, a six-year-old couldn't keep up with our hiking pace. However, it was still good to see her awake and conscious for most of the day.

She was a calm child, always sitting still and content to be carried most of the time. That might have been due to the leftover fatigue from her illness, but there was an alert curiosity in her eyes as she watched the forest passing by around us.

CREED

As we traveled, I asked Robyn about his community. He told me about the people he'd grown up with, mostly adults. It was a varied mix. Some were kind, others not so much. Mostly interestingly, however, was the fact that, despite the Grieve family running the cult, there were only two Grieves left. Chester Grieve, the man that had imprisoned Kayden and me, and the man's son.

Chester Grieve's son was already approaching middle age, and so far, he hadn't managed to have any children, despite having several wives. If he didn't manage to reproduce soon, the Grieve family might be coming to an end, and there had been a lot of squabbling among the adults about who would take over leadership if that happened.

As far as I was concerned, that bloodline couldn't die out soon enough.

We passed the next two days of our trip without much trouble. When we reached a break in the trees, and the town of Whimborne came into view, I dared to feel hopeful.

If we could just find a phone in town to call Brody and Magnus, then we had a good chance of getting out of this without encountering our captors again.

Whimborne was a small place, barely worthy of being called a town. Most of the roads weren't even paved, and the buildings looked like they hadn't been properly refurbished since the pioneer days. It was our best chance of going unnoticed by our pursuers, who would likely assuming we were headed for one of the larger towns nearby. However, in a small place like this we were also more likely to be noticed by the locals.

"Wait here," I told Kayden, who was crouching with the children in the shadows at the edge of town. "I'm going to go find a phone. I shouldn't have to go far, but if I don't come back in the next few minutes, find a place to hide yourselves and wait for Magnus and Brody to come get you."

Just as I turned away from them, a hand tugged at my sleeve.

"Mister Creed," Robyn said as he looked up at me, his voice small but steady. "Let me come with you."

Although he was twelve, just one year from being a teenager, Robyn was small for his age. I had to kneel to be on level with him.

"It'll be safer for you to stay here with Kayden."

He immediately shook his head. "No, I should come with you. I know all the people from my community. I'll recognize them easier."

The kid had a point. Other than the individuals who kidnapped us, I hadn't met most of the members of the cult.

With a sigh of resignation, I nodded. "All right, you can come with me. But if I tell you to run, then you run, all right?"

The boy nodded and stood up as straight as he could, like he was about to charge into battle. "I got it."

"All right. Let's go."

I shared one last look with Kayden as he cradled Mavis in his arms, then turned and left with Robyn right on my heels.

The two of us slunk up to the backside of a building at the very edge of town. Made from old brown brick, it looked like it would fall down at any moment, but from the activity I could hear just out of sight, the place still seemed to be functioning. It was a post office, as far as I could tell, with several large garage doors in the back for accepting deliveries.

More importantly, however, there was a ladder just off to the side of the garage door that led up to the roof.

"Come on," I said to Robyn, pointing at the ladder. "Up here. We'll be able to get a better look at the area from the roof."

CREED

The first few rungs of the ladder had rusted away, so I had to pick Robyn up for him to reach the higher ones. I kept him in front of me as we climbed, making sure he didn't fall. When we reached the roof, we found one of the first signs of modernization on the town. The roof was metal, instead of the worn tile that I had expected, and a satellite dish stood proudly pointing toward the sky.

That was a good sign. A satellite dish meant the building was connected to the rest of the world. We had a good chance of finding a phone to use here.

After instructing Robyn to stay low, the two of us crawled on our stomachs to the edge of the roof. Most of the buildings in the town weren't more than a couple stories high, so we had a good view of everything. The roads of the town had a circular design, like the spokes of a wheel radiating from a central point. A few people walked along the street, ambling casually as though they were in no rush to get wherever they were going. One person was talking on a cellphone, waving animatedly with their other arm. I was half tempted to climb down from our hiding place and steal the phone from them.

No, that wouldn't be a good idea. Not only would it draw a lot of attention to us, but most modern phones required a passcode anyway. I could bypass the average phone's security system, but it would require tools I didn't currently have. Unless I got lucky enough to grab the phone right out of their hands while they were still using it, stealing the cell phone wouldn't do me much good.

A sharp poke against my arm caught my attention.

"Mister Creed," Robyn said as he urgently jabbed at me. "Look."

He pointed toward a car sitting on the side of the road near the center of town.

"I know that car."

I squinted against the afternoon sunlight in the car's direction. "Are you sure?" It was a silver, four-door sedan, no different than any other car and as forgettable as a car could be. Yet, Robyn nodded with absolute certainty.

"See that dent in the back fender? My sister and I accidentally did that when we were riding our bicycles and ran into it. My sister put a sticker of a kitten over the dent, because she thought it would work like a Band-Aid."

Looking again, I noticed the sticker that he was talking about. From a distance, it was little more than a white dot on the car's silver surface, but the dot was in the recognizable shape of a cat.

"So, that car belongs to someone from your community?"

Robyn nodded again.

I bit my lip to keep from cursing out loud.

The cult had already caught up to us. That was the problem when running from an enemy that had so many more people than you. They could afford to send out search parties in all directions rather than trying to follow you directly.

There was no point in leaving. We'd probably find cult members in every nearby town.

"Okay, let's think," I muttered to myself.

The town wasn't very big. It would take almost no time for our pursuers to search every nook and cranny of the place. Whatever we were going to do, we had to do it soon.

A rumbling sound drew my attention away from the silver car of our pursuers. A pair of delivery trucks pulled up behind the post office, slowly backing themselves up to the garage doors. Robyn and I watched from the roof as cartful after cartful of packages, all different sizes of brown cardboard boxes, were hauled off the truck. The post office seemed to be short staffed, so the process took a while, giving me plenty of time to think.

Since Whimborne was so remote, it had to get a lot of its supplies delivered. The post office was one of the few thriving parts of the town, and most importantly, the most modern. They had a satellite dish. They were connected.

Each package had its own label with a barcode specifically for keeping track of it.

Off to the side of the garage sat another pile of packages. This one was much smaller than the number of incoming packages and were labeled as "outgoing".

An idea came to me.

"Okay, Robyn, here's what we're going to do," I told the boy. "We wait for them to finish unloading those trucks, and then we're going to climb down there. While I handle things here, I need you to run back to Kayden and your sister and tell them to meet us here immediately. Got it?"

With a very serious look on his face, Robyn silently nodded.

It took another few minutes, for both trucks to finish being unloaded. After that, the drivers and unloaders went back inside the main building, probably to handle whatever paperwork was required for the delivery.

Robyn and I took the opportunity to climb down from the roof. He took off running in the direction where we'd left Kayden and Mavis, while I headed for the stack of "outgoing" boxes.

Selecting one from the top of the pile, I headed for the payphone hanging on the wall.

Luckily, Robyn had included a bit of cash in the supplies that he'd brought along. Otherwise, without quarters for the phone, this whole plan would have fallen apart.

The phone picked up on the first ring.

"Hello?" Brody's voice echoed through the line, distorted by static and white noise.

"Brody," I said urgently. "Write this down."

Anyone else would have demanded to know what was going on, but as soon as he heard my voice, Brody was all business. He didn't say a single thing as I read out the number on the package that I held.

"That's the tracking number for a package. Come find it." Voices alerted me that the delivery drivers were already returning. "Hurry up."

Then I slammed the phone back on its receiver. I had about thirty seconds to find a hiding place before the drivers returned. Not enough time to get back to the roof. Instead, I tossed the package I was carrying back into the "outgoing" pile, then crammed myself into a metal storage locker. Hopefully, none of the supplies inside the locker would be needed, because if anyone opened it, I had no place to run.

Through slats in the front of the storage locker, I watched as the drivers and loading staff carried the "outgoing" packages onto the trucks. The package whose number I'd given to Brody was on the top of the stack, so it was one of the first to be loaded onto a truck.

Specifically, the right truck.

Great, now I just needed to get Kayden, myself, and the kids onto the truck. Then we'd not only have an escape vehicle, but also a way for Brody and Magnus to track us. If everything went according to plan, they'd meet us at the truck's next stop.

When the trucks were loaded up, the drivers climbed into the front seat. It was now or never.

Climbing out of the storage locker, I hoped Robyn had been successful.

I was careful to stay out of the line of sight of the drivers and I poked my head out of the garage, looking out at the line of trees not far away.

From under the cover of a large bush, I saw Kayden waving me down.

His movements were conspicuous. He was going to be spotted, and a man hiding in the forest with two children would seem suspicious no matter how you looked at it.

Unable to explain my plan, I hastily waved him over to me. Thankfully, he complied without hesitation and met me beside the garage with both kids.

"Creed? What are we doing?"

"Get in the truck."

"What? But—"

There wasn't time to explain, and I cut him off by turning away and headed to the back of the truck we needed. It was locked, but the lock was old and easily gave way to the lock pick that I'd prepared earlier.

Just as the truck rumbled to life, I pulled up the rolling door just high enough for Kayden and the kids to squeeze under.

"Get in."

Kayden hesitated a moment. He still didn't know what I was doing, and from his perspective this probably seemed like insanity.

I implored him with my eyes to trust me.

Swallowing down his obvious nerves, Kayden brought the kids over to the truck.

"All right. You two. Get on."

Together, we piled the kids into the truck. By then, the first of the two trucks pulled out of the garage. Our truck would soon follow, so there will wasn't time for me to explain my plan to Kayden. I just shoved him toward the opening in the door and implored him to get on.

He had to lie on his stomach and slide himself under the door, similar to how he'd gotten past the fence surrounding the cult, but this time I made sure to leave enough room for him.

I was just about to follow, when the sound of shouting caught my attention.

The first truck had been stopped by a familiar silver car blocking its path. I didn't recognize any of the people that climbed out of the car, but I understood well enough when they started demanding to search the truck.

They didn't even know for certain that we were in this town, but these cult members were certainly thorough with their search.

It was too optimist to think that they might search the first truck and be satisfied. They were going to search the second one, too, and when they did, they would find us.

Coming to a quick decision, I grabbed one of the packages off the truck that was about the size of a book—after making sure that it wasn't the same package whose number I'd given to Brody—and tucked it under my arm.

"Stay on this truck until it reaches its next destination, then get off. Try to make sure no one sees you."

Kayden opened his mouth to demand what was going on, but I closed the door before he could say a word.

Hoisting the package that I held a little higher in my arm, I took a deep breath and stepped out from behind the truck.

I stuck to the wall, sneaking around in an over-exaggerated fashion that made me feel like a cartoon. It took longer than I thought it would, but eventually, they noticed me. I kept my body angled toward them that would show off the package that I held under my arm, hoping that from a distance it would be mistaken for a journal.

My rouse seemed to work, because the cult members started shouting to each other to catch me. Once I was certain that they had abandoned their plan to search the trucks, I took off running back into the cover of the forest.

It felt like I'd stepped back in time, before my retirement from the military, when carrying out dangerous missions was part of my everyday life. Running through the wilderness on my own, enemies in hot pursuit, and nothing but the clothes on my back for supplies. It wasn't fun, but it was comfortable in its familiarity.

I could do this.

I could keep our enemies occupied long enough for Kayden and the kids to get to safety.

Too bad it was the middle of the day. This would have been much easier at night, but I couldn't make the earth turn any faster.

My feet still remembered their agility as I darted between the trees, stepping over twisted roots and vaulting over large rocks. Branches whipped at my face and arms, threatening to slow me down.

Behind me, just far enough to be out of sight, I could hear the sounds of people chasing me. They crashed through the underbrush like bulldozers, not even bothering to find the easiest path as they carved their own route through the forest.

I could also hear the howling of dogs. It was as I'd feared before, they'd brought scent hounds with them. It was expected for a remote cult that probably did a lot of its own hunting, but also annoying.

Escaping them would be a lot harder with trained beasts on my heels.

My thoughts cast back to Kayden.

"Please be safe," I whispered as I slowed down. I kept running, but now it was more of a light jog than a sprint.

If I got too far away, they might give up on me and go back for Kayden. It was a delicate balance. I couldn't let them actually catch me, but I had to stay close enough to give them a reason to keep chasing.

At least until we were deeper into the mountains.

After about an hour, and covering several miles of distance, I decided it was enough. We were far enough away from town that my pursuers wouldn't be able to easily turn back.

Time to turn the tables on them.

Thanks to the maps that I'd memorized, and Lisianthus's journal, I knew that there was a rocky area coming up. Ancient rivers had carved deep channels into the earth, eventually drying up and leaving chasms with tall stone walls that snaked through this part of the mountain like creeping vines.

I ran down one of the old riverbeds, going just far enough to round a bend and disappear out of my pursuers' sight. Then I climbed up the chasm wall, digging my fingers into cracks in the rock and pulling myself upward until I reached the top. From there, I jumped down into another riverbed, and returned to my pursuers to once again get their attention. Those who hadn't already gone down the first riverbed quickly chased me down the second, effectively dividing their numbers in half.

In this way, I was able to scatter my pursuers among the natural maze of the ancient riverbeds. It gave me enough breathing room to start making an actual plan.

First, I needed a weapon. A gun or knife would have been preferable, but I wasn't going to just find either of those lying around the forest. Instead, I found an adequately sized stick and scrapped its end against a jagged edge of stone until I managed to make a rudimentary spear.

Second, I needed to start playing defense. They had an advantage of superior numbers. No matter how well I avoided them, I could only run for so long before they wore me down.

Sitting hunched down on a rocky ledge as I watched my pursuers in the riverbed below, I checked the watch on my wrist. It had been about two hours since I left Kayden. Assuming he was able to immediately get to a phone and call for help, then Magnus and Brody should only be a couple more hours away.

I could last that long.

One of my pursuers passed right below my hiding spot. In the past, I would have used this opportunity to take out one of my opponents while I could, but that was not the point of my mission right now. I didn't need to fight. I needed to survive.

The cult member continued down the

dry riverbed, their back exposed to me. It would have been a perfect opportunity, if killing them was my objective, but the large hunting dog walking by the man's side kept me from acting.

Just before they disappeared from sight, their phone rang, and they stopped right in the middle of the riverbed to answer it.

"Hey! Oh really. You found them. The other one and the kids. I mean, I guess it'll have to do. Maybe we can get something out of them."

I clenched my hand around my makeshift spear, and had to remind myself to keep breathing even as my mind kept screaming one word.

Kayden!

Absolutely not. I did not go through all of this just for Kayden to get caught anyway.

Jumping down from my hiding place, I tackled the man into the dirt. He didn't even have time to scream before I jammed the end of my sharpened stick into his shoulder.

Then he screamed, loud enough to startle the birds from the nearby trees.

"Where are they?" I practically spit in his face, kneeling over him to pin him down as I dug the stick harder into his shoulder.

The man squirmed and cursed as he clutched at the stick, trying to keep it from piercing any deeper. I watched in satisfaction as blood oozed from the wound and dripped onto the forest floor.

But then, terrifyingly, the man smiled up at me.

My instincts flashed a warning at me, begging me to run away, but before I could move, I felt a prick in the side of my neck. Reaching up, I pulled a familiar dart out of my flesh.

Fuck.

It was a trap.

They'd pretended to find Kayden to lure me out, and I'd walked right into it.

Dizziness immediately swarmed me, making the world around me seem to spin. I tried to run, but I didn't get more than two steps before my legs went numb and I fell. I didn't even feel it when my face slammed into the loose stones and dirt lining the riverbed. My consciousness fled and darkness consumed my vision, and last thing I noticed was the sound of approaching footsteps.

***

I awoke to a pounding headache and the feeling of cold metal around my wrist.

Not again, I groaned in my head while on the outside I didn't utter a sound.

"Awake?" the familiar voice of Chester Grieve asked.

Even though I hadn't reacted in any way, not even opening my eyes, he somehow knew the moment I returned to consciousness.

I still didn't bother to open my eyes, not wanting to give him the satisfaction, and simply said "Fuck off."

The other man merely chuckled. "Oh, I will, shortly. I can assure you that."

Now that I was more awake, I realized I felt strange. My mouth was dry, and my nerves buzzed under my skin. This wasn't just the after effects of being knocked unconscious. Something was wrong.

Finally opening my eyes, I wasn't surprised to find myself in a completely nondescript room. It wasn't the same room where Kayden and I had been locked up, but other than that, I had no idea where I was.

When I tried to sit up, I found my wrists handcuffed above my head, stretched out to either side. Based on the softness under me, I assumed I was lying on a bed, so my wrists must be attached to the headboard.

I glared at Chester Grieve with all the strength I could muster. "What did you do to me? Where's Kayden?"

Both questions practically spilled out of me at the same time, each equally important. I wasn't sure which I wanted him to answer first, but I was certain that I would hate anything he had to say.

The other man rocked back a bit in his wheelchair, almost looking like he was thinking. "I have no idea where your friend is, but he's of no concern. I'm more interested in you."

Rolling over to a side table just at the edge of my line of sight, he pulled out of folder from the drawer. I recognized the folder and wasn't surprised when he returned and held up photos of Lisianthus's journal for me to see.

"You took the journal with you, so I assume you've managed to crack the code and have some idea of what it said. Find anything interesting?"

I would have spit in the man's face if he was close enough, but I settled for a mocking smile. "Yes. I know what you're looking for. What the Milford sisters stole from you."

As expected, Chester Grieve's expression twitched with annoyance when he heard the name "Milford," but he didn't get angry like I'd hoped.

"Oh? So, the journal mentioned that?"

The chains on my wrists rattled as I tested their strength. "Yeah. Although, I gotta say. It's kinda misleading to say they stole from you. They just left. I'm sure, if they could have chosen not to be pregnant at the time, they would have."

I'd been shocked when I came to that part of the journal, but the more I thought about it, the more it made sense. All three sisters had been married off to the cult founder. It was no surprise that pregnancy would soon follow. The only shocking thing, aside from the girls' young age, was the fact that they'd all ended up pregnant around the same time.

No wonder they'd chosen to escape when they did. They were staring down the barrel of their future as a trio of baby factories for the cult, and they decided enough was enough.

As a man, I couldn't fully empathize with the difficulties of pregnancy, but it must have been difficult. Based on stories Brody and Magnus had told me about the *Mothers of the Mountain*, the three sisters hadn't been pregnant when they arrived in Emberwood.

Had they found somewhere safe to go, or had they stayed out there, alone, in the forest as each of them gave birth?

Either way, it must have been terrifying. I'd been through some difficult situations in my life, but that was one I couldn't imagine.

Chester Grieve tossed the photos aside. "So, you do know about it. Tell me, what did they do with the children? Did any of them survive?"

In reaction to his questions, I just laughed. It came out sounding more manic than I intended. I didn't feel fully in control of my body. Everything was too hot, and my brain felt like it was floating inside my skull. It almost seemed like I was drunk, except I knew I hadn't had a drop to drink.

"You're insane if you think I'll tell you anything. I know all about your little bloodline problem. You and your son are the only Grieves left, and its looking like your son is probably infertile. Once the two of you are gone, your bloodline is finished. You want to find out what happened to the Milford sister's children so you can track down any surviving members of your lineage. Well, too bad. I'm not going to help you drag any more innocent people into your little cult."

I expected anger. Maybe even threats

to try and force me to help him. I was prepared for it all. I'd been captured by enemies tougher than this. I'd even faced torture before. Whatever they had planned for me, I could take it.

What I was not prepared for was laughter.

"Oh, you'll help us," Chester Grieve said with a strange look in his eye. "We don't even need your cooperation."

Without warning, he suddenly ran a finger down the exposed skin of my arm. It was such a slight touch that I barely should have noticed it, but that barest friction of skin lit every nerve in my body on fire.

It didn't hurt, but it was so overwhelming that it left me writhing on the bed. The chains on my wrists rattled, but didn't budge.

Chester Grieve watched my reaction for a moment. "Hmm, yes. I think you're ready."

He rolled away from the bed toward the door, and I was left gaping at him, gasping for breath.

"Wha... what did you do to me?"

Rather than answer me, he opened the door and ushered someone inside. A young woman stepped through the door. At first, I feared she was a child. She looked young and had a very slim figure, almost bordering on underweight. However, when I got a closer look at her face, she looked a little older than a teenager. Probably early twenties.

She was also dressed in nothing but a satin robe.

God, please let her at least be in her twenties. I had no idea what Chester Grieve had planned for her, but whatever it was would be even worse if it turned out she was a child.

The poor thing was trembling like a leaf caught in a hailstorm. She clutched at the front of her robe, holding the thin material to her like it was a shield. She didn't even have any shoes to protect her feet, just that single piece of satin to keep her covered.

"Are you sure about this?" she asked Chester Grieve, even as her terrified gaze kept darting toward me.

He patted her on the arm. It was the kind of gesture that a kindly grandfather would do while comforting a scared child. Coming from this man, seeing him acting like that, made my stomach churn.

"I know it'll be hard," he said, his voice disturbingly soft. "But you must do it for our community. It's the only way we can secure our lineage."

"You're fucking crazy!" I shouted at both of them. "What's even the point? This isn't going to help you at all."

I tried to fight my way off the bed, lashing out with my legs as if I could kick myself free, only to find that my ankles were chained up as well. I was chained flat to the bed, unable to do more than writhe around.

"On the contrary," Chester Grieve said, sounding far too calm for the situation. "You're going to be a big help."

I glared at the terrified girl, but my vision swam the harder I tried to focus. My head felt like someone had replaced my brain with cotton. "If she's some relative of yours, why not just marry her off to another member of your cult? Why involve me at all?"

"Oh, no," Chester Grieve shook his head, even as he pushed the girl closer to the bed. "She isn't my relative. You are."

I could only gape at him, too stunned for words. My eyes bugged out of my head until they began to water, and I had no choice but to blink.

Yet, Chester Grieve acted as though he hadn't said anything weird. In fact, the man was so calm, that for a moment I wondered if I was the crazy one.

"I wasn't sure until I met you in person, but now I'm certain. Why else would three men randomly buy property in an area they had no connection to unless something in your blood called to it? It was instinct for you to return to the land of your ancestors, and you've come at just the right time to save us from decline. With your help, we can revitalize our community and return to our former glory."

The man was insane. There was no other explanation for it.

"Just because I bought the land that the Milford sisters used to own doesn't mean I'm related to them."

"That's why I said I wasn't sure until I met you." Chester Grieve shuffled the girl closer to the bed until she was only inches away from me. "According to our records, each of the triplet sisters was uniquely gifted. To grow, to build, and to survive. Those were the ideals that they brought to our community, and the three of you embody it so perfectly. It can't be a coincidence. This is the work of fate."

I strained against the chains hard enough to shake the whole bed, but it accomplished nothing. "Yes, it can be a coincidence. Coincidences happen all the time."

Realizing I wasn't going to be breaking free any time soon, I stopped fighting, but I didn't give up on the argument.

"Look, even if you were right, this isn't going to work. I'm... I'm gay. Very, very gay. So, it doesn't matter what woman you bring here, it really isn't going to work."

I'd hoped that Chester Grieve would at least hesitate over this wrench in his plan, but the man didn't even blink.

"Don't worry about that. We've already taken care of it. Eventually, we'll have to find a way to collect your friends as well, but for now, we can start with you."

The girl ran a tentative hand down my arm, and every nerve in my body lit up like someone had poured gasoline over me and lit a match. I felt like I was on fire and sweat started to bead on my forehead.

Even worse, I felt myself becoming aroused.

A horrifying realization settled over me. While I'd been unconscious, they must have drugged me with some sort of aphrodisiac. I really wasn't going to have a choice in this.

They wanted a child from me, and they were going to get it one way or another.

CHAPTER TEN

Kayden

THE FLOOR OF the delivery truck rattled around us, as the two kids and I sat huddled in the middle of stacks of cardboard boxes. I was trying not to panic as, with every second that passed, we grew farther and farther from Creed.

He hadn't even told me what his plan was. I could only assume that he had one, and trust that it would work. All he'd said was that I needed to stay on the truck and get off at the next delivery stop, so that's exactly what I was going to do.

Creed had our only watch, so there was no way for us to tell the time. Based on the sunlight I could see coming through the crack under the door, I guessed that a couple hours had passed. I fed the children a granola bar from our bag, but I wasn't hungry. My stomach rolled every time I thought about what might be happening to Creed, and I feared that if I tried to eat anything, I'd just throw it right back up.

Both Robyn and Mavis had nodded off leaning against my shoulder, and I was on the way to following them, when the feeling of the truck slowing down brought me back to attention. Our journey had been a smooth trip so far, barely ever turning or changing speed, but something had definitely changed.

Had we arrived somewhere, or where we just changing direction?

The truck took several turns, and even

came to a stop a few times, but it took several minutes before it came to a full stop and turned off.

We'd arrived at our destination, wherever that was. Whatever Creed's plan had been, I hoped it was about to pan out, because I didn't know what to do from here.

If I was smarter, I would have thought ahead, but I'd been so worried about Creed that I never considered what would happen when the truck came to a stop. Creed had said to try and stay out of sight, but the moment the delivery workers opened the door, they were clearly going to see us.

Looking around for a solution, the only thing at my disposal were the delivery packages. There weren't enough to hide all of us, but if I stacked them in the corner, I might be able to hide the kids for a bit.

It was the best plan I had, so I went

with it.

"Get behind here and stay quiet," I told the kids as I started stacking boxes. "I'm not sure what's going to happen, but if it looks like things are going bad, I'll create a diversion and you need to run, all right?"

Robyn clung to his sister, holding the small girl in his arms. "Where should we run?"

That was a good question. One I didn't have an answer to, but I couldn't tell the kids that. They were already scared enough.

"Um, you should probably head to the nearest police station."

Creed had said that the local authorities probably couldn't be trusted, but at that moment I could think of no better option. Hopefully, we'd get lucky and the police station in this town wouldn't be as corrupt as Creed feared.

"Okay," Robyn nodded very seriously.

"Where's that?"

Right. Telling them to go to the police station was no help when I wasn't even sure where we'd ended up. For all I knew, the truck had brought us to a large city, and the police station was miles away.

I could hear footsteps right outside the door. We only had a few more moments before we were discovered.

I wracked my brain for any advice I'd ever heard about what children should do if they were lost. Staying in one place and waiting for rescue was usually the answer, but that was mostly for if someone was lost out in the wilderness.

"Ah," I said as something finally came to me. "I got it. If you have to run, then you should go up to the first adult you see that has children with them and tell them you're lost. They should be able to then take you to the police station."

Was that right?

I'd read it on the Internet once. It

sounded right, but one never could tell with Internet advice.

The rolling door started to open. It was too late to second-guess myself now. I shoved both kids back behind the boxes as far as I could, and placed myself right in the middle of the truck so I was the first thing the delivery drivers would see. Hopefully, they'd be so surprised by my presence that they'd completely overlook the kids.

"What the..." one of the delivery drivers gasped when they saw me. "Who the hell are you? What are you doing in there?"

"Oh, well, you know," I stuttered and nervously scratched at the back of my head, hoping that I came off as awkwardly innocent. "I was on a camping trip and got lost out there. Then I saw this truck and I thought, hey, that should take me to a town somewhere. So, I jumped on. Sorry about bumming a free ride, but you really helped me out."

The delivery men were not moved by my innocent act—never mind the fact that it was mostly the truth—and stared at me with eyes narrowed in suspicion.

"The door into the truck was locked. How did you get on?"

Damn.

I was hoping they wouldn't notice that. Saying I picked the lock would just make me look suspicions, and it wasn't even true. Creed had been the one to pick the lock. I just hopped onboard.

With no other answer to give them, I just shrugged again. "I don't know what to tell you. It wasn't locked when I tried the door. Maybe someone forgot to lock it."

They didn't like this answer. Perhaps they were the ones who had been responsible for locking the door and didn't like that I implied they'd failed at the job, because my suggestion only made them angry. One of them grabbed me by the collar of my shirt and yanked me off the truck. I stumbled as I jumped down from the raised truck bed and fell to my knees on the concrete floor.

I groaned at the pain that shot through my knee. Getting older sucked, and ever since I turned forty, it seemed like I was constantly finding new aches and pains. My knee was definitely going to bother me for a while after this.

"Who are you?" the delivery driver demanded.

I raised up my hands, trying to show them that I meant no harm.

"Well, that's a funny story, too. See, I'm a travel writer, and I—"

I was cut off as the driver started shaking me. "Stop your babbling and give us a straight answer."

Almost as soon as he started shaking me, the driver's hands suddenly disappeared from my shirt, and I fell hard on my butt.

"That'll be enough of that," someone said.

Rubbing at my abused tailbone, I looked up to see Brody holding the driver up by the lapels, high enough that the man's feet didn't quite touch the ground.

"Hey, you okay?" another person asked.

At this point, I wasn't even surprised to see Magnus kneeling at my side.

"Yeah," I sighed as I stood up. "Just bruised all over."

The sudden appearance of Magnus and Brody had caused my brain to stall, but after a moment, it all suddenly returned to me. Like a delayed reaction, my calm demeanor suddenly turned to panic.

"Wait. Magnus? Brody? You're here. Where's Creed? Did you find him?"

The other two men shared a worried look. "No. He said to meet you here. Luckily, this truck was going in the right direction, so we could meet you halfway. Otherwise, it would have taken us a lot longer to reach you."

I grabbed each of their arms, shaking them without actually moving either of them to emphasize my panic. "Creed just ran off. I don't know what happened to him. If he hasn't contacted you by now, then he must have been captured again."

Brody dropped the man he was holding, and the delivery drivers ran off. Neither Brody nor Magnus even seemed to notice as they turned their full attention on me.

Magnus gripped my arm tightly. His hand nearly encircled my biceps, which was impressive considering I wasn't a small man.

"Tell us everything that happened. You two went on your trip, but when your return date rolled around and we didn't hear anything from you, we knew something must have gone wrong."

CREED

As quickly as possible, I recapped everything that had happened to us since we set off on our trip. It felt like so long ago that we were packing up for a regular camping trip, but thinking back on it, I realized that it had been less than two weeks.

"All of that just to make Creed translate Lisianthus's journal," Brody said once I'd finished. He was pacing back and forth, hand on his chin as he was deep in thought. "That seems excessive, although I suppose it depends on what they're looking for. Did you ever find out what the Milford sisters supposedly stole?"

Feeling dizzy after the stress of the last few minutes, my legs gave out and I sat on the bumper of the truck. "No. Chester Grieve obviously knew, but never said. Although, I suspect Creed might have an idea. He suddenly got squirrely about the contents of the journal while we were escaping and stopped talking about it. I think he might have figured something out, but I never asked."

Magnus's suddenly slammed his fist into the side of the tuck, denting the metal. "Forget about that. What matters is that Creed has been captured again. We need to find him before this cult decides he's not worth the hassle of keeping alive."

I looked back and forth between Magnus and Brody, hoping one of them would have an answer. "So, where do we go? Back to where they were keeping us before? I don't even know what direction it was. Creed planned out our whole escape route."

"Maybe," Brody said, though he didn't sound convinced. "But if Creed's already escaped from there once, they may not want to take him back there again. Is there any other place you can think of where this cult might take people? Any place they mentioned, even in passing?"

I shook my head, disappointed that I couldn't give them a better answer, but when I opened my mouth to tell them this, another voice spoke in my place.

"The lake house."

Magnus, Brody, and I all jumped at the unexpected sound of a child's voice. I'd completely forgotten about Robyn and Mavis, who were still waiting in the truck, and based on Magnus and Brody's surprise, they'd also overlooked that part of my story.

"The lake house?" I asked as asked as I looked up at the two kids in the truck.

Robyn smiled back at me from where he sat amid the boxes. "Yeah. It's a house, by a lake, that always belongs to the leader. Only the leader is allowed to go there. The adults say it's a spiritual retreat that the leader uses for isolated reflection, but I know our leader has taken people there before. Is that the kind of place you're talking about?"

One by one, I lifted the kids out of the tuck and set them down on the ground. "That is exactly the kind of place we're talking about. You don't happen to know where it is, do you?"

***

Robyn, it turned out, was not able to provide the lake house's exact location, but he was able to give a pretty accurate description. Based on this, Brody and Magnus were able to figure out which lake the house was likely located on, and we immediately headed there. The truck that Magnus and Brody had brought to come find me easily charged across the rugged mountain roads, like the machine itself was on a mission. Magnus and Brody sat in the front, silent but determined as they prepared to find their friend. Meanwhile, I sat in the backseat with the two kids, who fell asleep in my lap almost as soon as we started driving.

It had been a long couple of days. I didn't blame them for being tired. I was as well, and if I wasn't so worried about Creed, I would have joined them in sleep.

We found the lake right where it was supposed to be. It was a large body of water, but I couldn't see any signs of a house. We drove around the roads that encircled the lake, looking for any sign of a structure. Not all the roads went close to the lake, and there were large stretches where I couldn't even see the water through the trees. Even if there was a lake house out here, we might drive right past it without even knowing.

"Wait, what was that?" Brody said as he suddenly grabbed Magnus's arm, who was driving.

Without a word, Magnus immediately put the truck in reverse and backed down the road to try and see what had caught Brody's attention.

"There."

Brody pointed toward a small dirt road, barely visible between the trees. It wouldn't have looked any different than a hiking trail, except for the metal gate blocking the road. The metal had been painted green, so it blended right in with the scenery. I would never have seen it as we drove past.

Magnus slapped the wheel and turned the car toward the new road. "Glad to see you haven't lost those sniper eyes of yours, Brody. Someone get out there and move the gate so we can get through."

I was out the door before he'd even finished speaking. The gate was heavy, but luckily, it wasn't locked. I was able to drag it aside without too much trouble and let Magnus bring the truck through. Then, just to be safe, I closed it behind us. If any of the cult members were patrolling the area, then I wanted to make sure nothing looked out of place to alert them to our presence.

CREED

We drove a little way down the new road, when Brody told Magnus to pull the truck over.

"We should leave it here and approach on foot. That way we can surprise them."

Magnus found a break in the trees where it was dry and flat enough for him to take the truck off the road and parked it. We gathered up a few bushes and placed them in front of the truck to hide it. It was a rushed camouflage job, and anyone looking too closely was bound to notice the truck, but hopefully, we wouldn't need to sneak around for too long anyway.

"You two stay here," I told the kids right before we left. "We're going to lock the truck, so don't try to leave. Just stay right where you are, and we'll be back soon."

They both nodded at me with wide eyes and their mouths pinched in identical looks of concern. I hated leaving them alone in the middle of the forest, but there wasn't anything else to do with them.

If the cult members did come across the pair, surely, they wouldn't hurt a couple of kids. Robyn and Mavis were no danger to them.

It was with a guilty heart that I left the kids behind and approached the end of the road on foot along with Magnus and Brody.

When we reached the end of the road, we stopped and hunkered down in the underbrush. A cabin sat off in the distance, right on the water's edge. Several cars and trucks were parked around it, haphazardly scattered across the grass. A pair of armed men stood beside the door like security guards. I recognized one of them. It was the same man that we'd knocked out and locked inside our room when we escaped the first time.

"We're definitely in the right place," I whispered to Brody and Magnus.

Brody studied the cabin for a second, before announcing a plan. "All right, here's what we're going to do. I'm not sure how many people there are, so we have to be careful. Magnus and I will take down the guard, while, Kayden, you go inside. If there are any more armed cult members, then you come back out immediately, but if there aren't, then go ahead and find Creed."

"And what if Creed isn't here?" I asked.

Neither Brody nor Magnus answered me right away.

"We'll worry about that if it comes to it," Magnus said as he patted me on the shoulder. "Now, let us go first, and then you follow right behind."

From the cover of the underbrush, I watched as Brody and Magnus moved in tandem, circling around the cabin so they could sneak up from either side. The guards never saw them coming, and not a single weapon was drawn or fired. One moment the guards were alert but at ease, and the next moment Magnus and Brody were vaulting over the porch railing and tackling them to the floor.

Magnus punched his target square across the face, knocking the man out flat, while Brody locked his target into a chokehold.

I didn't wait around to see the end of the fight. Following my instructions, I ran right past them and into the cabin, on guard for anyone who might try to attack me.

Inside, the cabin was mostly empty, except for Chester Grieve, who sat near the fireplace drinking tea.

The cup slipped from his hands.

"What? No, you have to leave. You can't be here. Guards!"

I almost felt bad punching an old man in a wheelchair.

CREED

Almost.

Then I remembered everything that the man had done to us, done to Creed and Creed's friends, and my regret instantly vanished.

"I'm sorry," I said as I shook out my hand, standing over his unconscious body. "But fuck you."

That took care of that, but where was Creed?

The cabin was only a single story, and didn't have many doors. I tried them one by one, until I came to a door that was locked. Magnus or Brody could have probably picked the lock just like Creed could, but I was too impatient for that.

Instead, I reared back and kicked the door in.

What I found inside made me freeze on the spot.

Creed lay there, handcuffed to a bed, with a naked woman sitting on top of him. I noticed with some relief that his clothes were still on, but the way he was writhing around and groaning was borderline indecent.

I saw red.

Charging into the room, I grabbed the woman by the arm and yanked her off of him.

"What the fuck do you think you're doing?" I screamed at her.

She immediately crumpled to the floor like a broken doll, hands over her face as she trembled. My fury disappeared as swiftly as it came. The girl was younger than I thought, probably only a few years into adulthood, and she looked terrified.

From the defense ball she curled into, it also seemed like she expected me to hit her. Even in my anger, I could never stoop so low to hit someone who was cowering away from me.

For now, I ignored her and turned back to Creed.

"Creed, babe. It's okay. I'm here now.

You're fine."

He barely seemed to hear me, continuing to writhe on the bed and tug helplessly at the chains keeping him prisoner.

Searching the nearby side table, I found a key that looked like it would fit the cuffs on his wrist. As I was unchaining him, I finally got a closer look at his face. He was sweating, and his eyes were dilated so wide that his pupils had completely overtaken his irises.

"Oh, God. Creed, what did they give you?"

I never got an answer. The moment the cuffs were freed from his wrists, Creed latched onto me and pulled me down into a fierce kiss.

CHAPTER ELEVEN

Creed

EVERYTHING WAS SO hot. I was burning up from the inside, like someone had built a bonfire in my chest that was now burning me from the outside, too. My vision even seemed to swim from the miasma of the heat radiating off me.

There was a weight on top of me, though I couldn't concentrate enough to tell what it was. All I knew was that, although it felt good, I hated it. A hand tugged at my shirt, managing to undo the first few buttons, but then I thrashed as much as my restraints allowed, and those hands were forced to stop.

I couldn't even remember why the touch of those hands turned my stomach, but I'd survived this long by relying on my instincts, and I wasn't going to stop now.

I heard a bang from somewhere close by, and a moment later, the weight on top of me disappeared. Cool air rushed to replace the now empty space above me, and I took several deep breaths. The cool air helped soothe the fever in my skin, but it also caused a deep shiver to ravage my body. I couldn't stop shaking. It was even making the bed beneath me tremble.

Bed?

Yes, that was right. Some clarity returned to my mind. I was tied to a bed, and I'd been drugged. By whom, and for what reason, I still couldn't recall, but I was certain it didn't mean anything good.

It wasn't the first time I'd been drugged

against my will. When I'd been captured and kept as prisoner of war, they'd sedated me most of the time as well.

At least, they did when they weren't interrogating me.

Is that what this was?

A new form of interrogation?

Well, it wasn't going to work. I wasn't sure what my interrogators wanted to know, but I certainly wasn't going to give it to them.

Footsteps sounded near the bed. Someone was coming closer.

I prepared myself for whatever vile villain wanted to torment me with. It wasn't the first time. I would get through it, and then I'd find some way to escape and get revenge on them

Just survive.

The face that leaned into my view brought a rush of relief. I knew that face. The name eluded me for a moment, slipping across my brain like a fish gliding downstream, but I knew that face. It was a good face. A friendly face. Although the expression was currently twisted into a look of distress, the sight of that face still brought with it a sense of safety.

"Creed, babe. It's okay. I'm here now. You're fine."

Kayden.

The name burst through my mind, along with a chaotic mix of images from our longstanding friendship. Everything, from our first meeting as children to our recent, more intimate, exchanges, played out behind my eyes all at once.

The restraints around my wrists fell away, but I barely noticed. As soon as I was free to move, I reached out, grabbed Kayden, and kissed him. I poured every ounce of relief I felt into that kiss.

If he was here, that meant I wasn't in danger. Everything would be fine.

Kayden returned the kiss, which was a relief, but it also ignited the smoldering embers of the drug in my chest. Fire licked through my veins once more, and I moaned deep in my throat.

Twisting my fists into his shirt, I tried to pull him onto the bed with me.

It didn't work. Kayden fought back and removed my hands from his clothing.

"No, Creed. Wait. We need to get you out of here."

I moaned again and tried to reach for him. We had a perfectly good bed right here.

Why wait?

It certainly had to be better than doing it in an unstable tent out in the middle of the wilderness.

Yet, despite my usually quick reflexes, he easily dodged me.

"Hold on, let me get you untied," he said.

I supposed that made sense. It would be a lot harder to do anything while I was still tied up.

I waited until my legs were free, and I tried to sit up and reach for him again. However, the moment my body was vertical, everything around me spun on its axis. I could no longer tell up from down, and my balance disappeared. I slid right off the edge of the bed and collapsed into a heap on the floor, clutching my head to keep it from spinning right off my shoulders.

"Oh, God! Creed. Are you okay?"

Kayden's ran his hands over me, checking for injuries, but even that touch felt good, cooling. Maybe it wasn't such a bad idea just staying on the floor. It was almost as comfortable as the bed, and the world didn't spin so much down here.

"Hey, I need some help," Kayden continued to shout. "Where are... Oh, Brody, how long have you been standing there?"

Brody was here?

That probably meant Magnus was here

as well. Everything would definitely be okay if they were here. Although, I didn't want an audience. I hadn't even told them about my relationship with Kayden. I'd barely even admitted to them that I was gay. They knew, of course, in the same way that I knew about them, but it had always been an unspoken thing between us. I was barely willing to admit it to them out loud, let alone let them see me with Kayden.

As these thoughts raced through my head, the conversation continued above me.

"What are you..." Kayden's voice trailed off, sounding confused. "Why are you recording? How long have you been doing that?"

"Since we got here," Brody said, his voice stern and matter of fact. "We're going to need evidence to prove what this cult did to us, otherwise they'll just be able to go free and continue harassing us.

This needs to end now."

Kayden sighed, and I felt the ghost of his breath against the back of my neck.

"Fine, but can someone help me with him? We need to get him out of here. I don't... I don't know what they did to him, but he's clearly been drugged."

More words were exchanged, and it was arranged that Magnus would take Kayden and I... somewhere, while Brody stayed behind to take care of things here.

I should have paid more attention. "Take care of" could have a lot of different meanings. It could mean that Brody would contact authorities to handle things, or it could mean that he simply planned to kill everyone involved. Either option was possible.

I should care. Even when we were all serving together, I hated the idea of my friends killing people for my sake. However, at the moment all I could feel was a sense of relief and security that someone else was taking charge. I could finally relax and focus on my important things.

Like how to convince Kayden to get back on the bed with me.

To my dismay, instead of returning to the bed, Kayden and Brody worked together to help me off the floor and herded me out the door. I was unstable on my feet, and they had to practically carry me with one arm draped over each of their shoulders.

The fresh air outside hit me like freight train, and I nearly collapsed on the spot into a shivering mess.

"Fuck," Kayden gasped as he was suddenly forced to bear more of my weight. "Seriously, what did they give him? I'm not sure we're going to be able to get him out of here."

"I can answer that," Magnus's voice reached us. "Here, look."

It was just as I suspected, if Brody was

here, then Magnus was as well. There was no doubt that the two would come for me, just as there was no doubt that I would come for them if the situation were reversed.

I was too busy staring at the ground, desperately hanging onto consciousness, to look up, but I could still hear what everyone was saying.

"What is that?" Kayden asked, sounding both curious and horrified.

"I think it's the drug they gave him," Magnus answered.

There was a shuffling sound as the people above me moved around, possibly passing the drug between them. Then, a moment later, Brody suddenly cursed.

"Fuck. I recognize this. Seriously, of all the drugs... There are better options if they just need an aphrodisiac."

Kayden's hand gripped my shoulder even tighter. I was kneeling on the ground, barely able to breathe without panting, but he'd never once let me go.

"What's wrong? Is he going to be okay?"

"It won't kill him, but..." Brody hesitated, and I knew whatever he was about to say wasn't going to be good. "Most drugs like this will eventually wear off over time, but not this one. There isn't even an antidote. The only way to make the symptoms stop it is..." He paused again, but this time the silence sounded different, more charged. "Relieve them."

The moment to catch my breath had helped, and I was starting to feel a little better. Not great, but there was a chance I could at least stand up without the world spinning around me.

Sensing my shift in movement, Kayden looped his hand under my arm again, prepared to help me stand up.

"I guess they really wanted to make sure they got a kid out of him." Kayden laughed, keeping his tone light, but there was a strain to his voice. "Well, that's not so bad. It's easily fixable, at least."

Between the three of them, they were able to haul me over to the truck they'd used to get here. There was a moment of confusion, as they'd actually left the truck near the beginning of the road, and someone had to run back to fetch it and bringing it closer, but once the vehicle was parked in front of me, I practically collapsed into back seat.

Every touch against my skin had been heightened a hundredfold. The upholstery of the truck's seat was probably usually very soft, but now it felt like sandpaper against my skin. Even my own clothes, which were thankfully still intact other than a few missing buttons from my shirt, were too much for me to bear. I was already reaching for my shirt, determined to remove it entirely, when a small voice stopped me.

"Mister Creed, what's wrong?"

CREED

A pair of inquisitive eyes were watching me from the front seat.

Oh, fuck.

The kids were in the truck. I'd completely forgotten about Robyn and Mavis. There was no way I could let the kids see me in such a state.

Instead of removing my shirt, I clutched the fabric tighter around my throat to try and hide my flushed skin as much as possible, and kept my hips angled down toward the seat so they couldn't see the evidence of my arousal.

"It's fine. I'm just... a little under the weather."

It took everything I had to keep my voice from shaking.

"That's right," Kayden agreed as he opened the passenger door. "He's a bit sick, so we're going to take him to a doctor to help him get better. That means I need you two to stay here for a bit. My friend, Brody, is also going to be staying here with you, so he'll take care of you while we're gone."

The kids tried to protest, but Kayden was already lifting Robyn out of the truck. It took some convincing, but eventually, the kids were left with Brody, while Magnus got behind the wheel and started the ignition.

Kayden was about to climb into the back seat with me, when I grabbed his arm and stopped him.

"You should ride up front."

He stared at me in confusion for a second, before a light of understanding flickered behind his eyes. If Kayden was too close to me, I may not be able to control myself, and Magnus was right there in the front seat. I may be a little more comfortable with my sexuality now, but I was definitely not interested in exhibitionism.

Despite it being my own request, I still struggled to let go of Kayden once I had a hold of him. He had to forcefully remove my hand from his arm, then, with one last uncertain look, he climbed into the front passenger seat.

I was left alone, sprawled face down on the back seat as the truck drove down the rough terrain of the mountain's backroads. There was no way to get comfortable. Every bump that the truck hit caused me to slide a bit against the seat, and the friction of the seat's upholstery against my skin nearly had me moaning obscenely. I had to bite my lip until it bled to keep myself quiet.

I barely remembered the drive. I was so focused on controlling my reactions, that I may as well have been unconscious. We could have driven to the other side of the country, and I wouldn't have noticed, I was so lost inside my own head.

My awareness of my surroundings came and went in waves. Sometimes, I would notice that the truck was completely silent, and sometimes there would be voices talking quietly.

One time I came back to awareness and found a very strange conversation happening. It took me a while to realize that I was the topic of the conversation, but I hoped that neither Magnus nor Kayden had anything negative to say.

"Creed doesn't trust people easily," Magnus was saying while keeping his eyes on the road. "So, it says a lot that he trusts you. That must mean that you're a good person. However, I still have to make one thing clear." He took his eyes off the road just long enough to stare at Kayden. It was just a brief glance before he had to turn his gaze back to the uneven road, but that brief second of eye contact would be enough to make a grown man fear for his life.

"If you hurt him, the police will never find your body."

With a solemn nod, Kayden raised

three fingers near his temple. "A Scout's Honor probably doesn't mean much coming from me since I was only a scout for, like, two weeks, but it's the best I can do. I promise I won't hurt him. He's been my closest friend for almost as long as I can remember. Even when he was serving overseas, when I thought he was straight and I didn't have a chance, his well being always came first for me. Nothing will change that."

I never heard Magnus's response. That was as long as my awareness lasted. Like a tidal wave crashing against the beach, I was pulled under the tide of my own desires again, and it took everything to keep myself still and quiet in the backseat.

The next time I realized what was happening around me, I was being hauled out of the truck. I struggled for a moment, thinking I'd been kidnapped again, until I recognized Kayden and Magnus beside me. They brought me out of the truck and into a motel room, where I was promptly dumped onto a piece of furniture that was almost too hard to be called a bed.

"Sorry about the shabby accommodations," Magnus said as he closed the front door behind us. "But I figured this was better than dragging you through a hotel lobby. Maybe it would have been better to stay at the lake house, after all. The bed would at least be more comfortable."

Magnus was talking to me, but I couldn't do much more than grunt, so Kayden responded for me.

"I don't think either of us would feel comfortable in the place where Creed was kept captive," he insisted, lingering near the bed but not touching me more than necessary. "This'll be fine. At least it'll be better than being out in the middle of the woods."

Magnus raised an eyebrow, and based

on what I knew of him, I was fairly sure he desperately wanted to ask if the two of us ever had sex out in the woods, but he restrained himself. With a few last awkward words, he explained that he'd be staying out in the truck until we were ready to leave.

Then he shut the door behind him, and Kayden and I were alone.

I should have been ecstatic. Ever since our first time together, back on the first night of our original hiking trip, I'd been looking forward to finally spending time with him back in civilization, with a proper bed and a room around us that wouldn't collapse at the slightest gust of wind.

But this was not how I wanted it to happen.

Reaching out, I tugged at his wrist.

"I'm sorry."

"Hey, no." He quickly sat on the bed beside me and took my hand within his own. "None of this is your fault."

"This isn't..." The words died on my tongue. I couldn't find the right thing to say. In frustration, I let my face fall back onto the bed and spoke directly into the mattress. "You deserve better than this."

Kayden's hand pressed against the back of my neck. "I deserve you, and that's what I've got. Now, you're burning up. We need to take care of this drug in your system."

He rolled me over onto my back and started unbuttoning my shirt. Even this small skin-to-skin contact, as his fingers brushed against my chest, sent thrills of pleasure up my spine. But with a desperate surge of energy, I grabbed his hands to stop him.

"No, it shouldn't... you shouldn't be obligated to do this."

I thought I was being considerate, but Kayden just laughed at me and batted my hands away so he could remove my shirt.

"Creed, being with you is never an obligation. This is something I'd want to do regardless. I'm just glad I can help you so easily. Now, lie back and let me take care of you."

With a deft agility that honestly surprised me, he removed the rest of my clothes before I even realized what was happening. The air on my naked skin was like a cold glass of water on a hot day, refreshing and satisfying in a way that I hadn't realized was possible.

But it didn't stop there.

Once I was undressed, his own clothing was quickly discarded as well. All the lights in the motel room were still on. I could see every inch of him better than every before, and I wanted him.

My mouth ran dry, and I reached for him, but he slapped my hands away and pinned them to the bed,

"No. You relax. I said I'd take care of you and that's exactly what I'm going to do.”

While locking eyes with me to ensure that I followed his direction and stayed still, he slid down my body until he was lying between my legs.

At first, his lips and tongue were gentle on my skin, kissing and licking everywhere except my desperately throbbing cock. It seemed like he was trying to gauge how sensitive I was, but the butterfly touches were driving me crazy and making the heat in my skin burn even hotter.

“Don’t tease,” I said through gritted teeth. “I can’t take it.”

“Sorry,” he whispered against my skin, though he didn’t sound the least bit apologetic. “I didn’t want to overwhelm you, but I won’t make you wait any longer.”

He immediately made good on his word. Without another moment of hesitation, his mouth descended on me and swallowed me whole. As his head bobbed up and down on my cock, I had to close my eyes to block out the sight. I was already so close to the edge, that it would take very little to tip me over the edge, and I wanted to enjoy it for at least a little while.

Kayden's attention was too good to rush.

Despite my best efforts, I still couldn't last very long. Not when my blood was boiling inside my skin and even the very air in my lungs seemed over-sensitive. Before I knew it, I was coming down his throat with a shout. My whole body shook from the force of it, and when the pleasure finally subsided, I collapsed onto the bed in a sweaty, panting mess.

I was still hard. Despite how good Kayden's mouth on me felt, the drug in my system still wouldn't let go. The aftershocks of my orgasm were still singing through my body, and I already wanted to go again.

"Hmm, someone's definitely eager," Kayden said when he noticed my aroused state. He idly stroked my cock a few times, and even just that much was enough to send my whole body thrashing.

He let go of my erection and then pressed a kiss to my forehead.

"Don't worry. I'll take care of you. Just give me a minute to get ready."

At some point while I'd been fading in and out of consciousness in the car, Magnus must have stopped at a store, because Kayden held up a plastic shopping bag that I hadn't noticed before. He dumped the newly bought condoms and lube onto the bed and started tearing open the packages.

I should have helped him, but my thoughts were swimming inside my head like my brain had turned to soup. All I could do was lie there and watch him as he rolled a condom over my cock before using the lube to prepare himself.

It was an attractive sight. Better than any porn I'd dared to watch. I wished I could have appreciated it more, but I was too eager to finally sink my aching cock inside him to think about anything else.

Soon, but not soon enough, he was straddling me. My arousal rubbed against his ass, desperate to push inside. Kayden ground his hips against me, once again teasing me despite the fact that he said he wouldn't.

I moaned and gripped his thighs so hard I probably left my fingerprints bruised into his flesh.

"Kayden," I gasped. "Please."

"I'm sorry. I'm sorry," he said, though he was clearly holding back laughter. "You're just too fun to tease. I can't help myself."

I gripped his thighs tighter, wishing I had enough coordination to just grab his hips and thrust myself inside him.

Luckily, he didn't keep me waiting too long. Still straddling me, he reached behind himself and took my cock in hand to help guide me to the correct spot.

An unwanted thought flashed through my head. This was a very similar position to the one I'd been in while handcuffed to the bed at the lake house. My hands were free this time, but they were so useless to me as may as well be restrained.

The only real difference was the identity of the person on top of me. The random young girl that had been forced into the room with me was completely unwanted. Even just thinking of her touch now sent shivers of revulsion snaking up my spine.

However, looking up at Kayden, with his lips still wet from the blowjob he'd given me and an attractive pinkish blush spreading all the way down his neck to his chest, I didn't want to be anywhere else.

When he finally sank down on me, it felt like coming home. The heat in my blood finally receded to a tolerable level, and I could think clearly for the first time since waking up chained to a bed.

Kayden's movements were slow and precise as he raised himself up as far as he could, only to then drop down quick so that I slid into him all at once, eliciting a groan from my throat. Over and over, he rode me with a steady, unending persistence. I held onto him with gentle hands, feeling each movement of his hips and basking in the ecstasy written on his face. Every little sound he made caused a new thrill of arousal to bury itself deep in my gut. My climax built within me, driving me higher and higher as Kayden's body milked every last drop of pleasure from me that it could.

I came with a silent shout. My throat was too dry to form words, but I still threw back my head as every muscle in my body contracted all at once like I'd been electrocuted. Kayden mumbled something to me as he continued to ride me through the pleasure, reaching his own end at nearly the same time, spilling his heat over my belly.

The overwhelming sensations lasted so long, and faded so gradually, that it never really felt like it ended. One by one, my muscles slowly relaxed until I lay like a limp noodle draped over the bed. Gasping for breath, Kayden collapsed and joined me, lying by my side with both arms and legs wrapped around me like he never intended to part from me again.

"Are you... feeling better?" he asked, panting against my shoulder.

"Perfect," I sighed.

I started to roll over, intending to kiss him, when I was stopped by an unexpected sensation.

We both looked down in surprise.

I was still hard. While I felt satisfied

after the intense pleasure that Kayden had wrung out of me and would have been happy to simply spend the rest of the night holding him, the drug in my system apparently had other ideas.

A flush of heat spread across my face, and I knew it was so bright that I could almost see a red glow reflecting off Kayden's skin. I was mortified. Kayden had already done so much for me. Surely this was asking too much.

But what else could I do?

According to Brody, the effects of the drug wouldn't just go away on their own. I had no choice but to ask for Kayden's help.

Before I could say anything, Kayden just laughed as he leaned forward to kiss me.

"Looks like our night isn't over."

***

It was an awkward ride home. At least for

me. Once the danger of the cult had been dealt with, Magnus and Brody weren't shy about cracking jokes at my expense. They apparently found the idea of me being drugged by the world's most powerful aphrodisiac hilarious, and Kayden also eagerly joined in on the humor. I was apparently the only one who found the whole incident embarrassing, though I couldn't regret the outcome. Kayden had proved himself reliable in the eyes of Magnus and Brody, and they now accepted him into our rapidly growing group.

Well, at least *The Tamed Souls* cult wouldn't be bothering us any longer.

While I'd been... preoccupied, Brody had also been busy. He'd contacted several local authorities, including Deputy Hillard, who had helped him gather as much evidence as possible against the cult. My kidnapping case had eventually ended up in FBI hands, as apparently the cult had dealings across state lines.

The evidence of my kidnapping, along with Robyn and Mavis's testimony for the rampant abuse within the cult, was a base for a strong case. Even if the cult was able to fight the charges, it was going to keep them distracted for a long time. We likely wouldn't be hearing from them any time soon.

Robyn and Mavis were taken into state custody. They were going to be placed in the care of a foster family, but I also vowed to keep an eye on them. I owed a lot to those kids and if the family they ended up with turned out to be a bad one, I would not hesitate to take custody of them myself.

For now, however, they seemed to be in good hands.

Upon our arriving back home, Trent and Ellis were ecstatic to see us. It had been a long time since I had anyone to come home to, even on a platonic level.

Brody and Magnus were usually out on the same missions with me, so we usually all returned home together.

It was something I could get used to.

The six of us sat around Brody's kitchen table, one of the few pieces of furniture large enough for all six of us, and Kayden and I explained everything that had happened to us since we left nearly two weeks ago.

We spared no detail, and the explanation took a couple hours. We ended up stopping halfway through to make dinner, which turned out to be a small feast when feeding all six of us. The remnants of the meal still sat on the table—and a few plates had even ended up on the floor for the dogs to lick clean— when our story finally came to an end.

"So, is it really over?" Ellis asked as he hand fed Indigo pieces of chicken from his own plate.

In answer, Brody and Magnus both

spoke at the same time.

"Yes."

"No."

The two looked at each other in confusion.

"It's over," Brody insisted. "You were busy at the time, but I helped collect the evidence myself. Blatant kidnapping like that is a serious crime, especially if it's getting kicked all the way up to a federal level. The cult may still exist, but they won't be coming after us anymore. We have nothing for them."

Huffing in exasperation, Magnus haphazardly stacked a few of the empty plates and started carrying them over to the sink.

"We do have something they want. You heard that Grieve guy. He really thinks we're the descendants of the *Mothers of the Mountain* and *The Tamed Souls* founder. That kind of delusional fanaticism doesn't just go away. Besides, we don't have all the answers yet."

Everyone else, including Kayden, rose to help clear the table. I tried to help as well, but I was told to stay put and take it easy. Apparently, although they were happy to joke about me being kidnapped and drugged, they were also worried about me.

If it meant I didn't have to do dishes, then I was happy to let them spoil me a bit longer.

"What do you mean we don't have all the answers?" Trent asked as he brought another stack of dishes to the sink.

Magnus moved on to packing away the leftover food into containers so it could be refrigerated for later. His focus remained on his task, so he couldn't look up, but he still addressed the question.

"The dowel we found in the underground vault. We still don't know the meaning of that."

Brody took the newly emptied plates

from him and began rinsing them off before piling them into the dishwasher.

"I suppose you're right. If Chester Grieve thought the vault contained information about the children of their founder, then I can understand why he sent people to find it, and why they were so disappointed by the outcome. However, it doesn't explain why the vault was built in the first place or why it contained only a simple wooden dowel."

His voice and expression both had a sour edge to them, which was understandable. He and Ellis had also been captured in order to get into the vault, though not for as long as Kayden and I had been held hostage.

After the dishes were taken care of and the table was clear, Brody brought out the wooden dowel that had remained locked in the safe in his office all this time. It looked just as unremarkable as the last time I'd seen it. The piece of wood was clearly well crafted and carefully polished, but there was ultimately not a single noteworthy thing about it.

I also brought out Lisianthus's journal. I'd managed to get my hands on it when everything with *The Tamed Souls* case was wrapping up, and I'd managed to finish translating the rest of it. Nothing in the journal explained about the vault or the dowel, but it was the only other clue we had.

The dowel and the journal sat together on the table, looking completely out of place next to each other.

"Are you sure there wasn't anything in the journal that mentioned this?" Brody asked me, not for the first time.

I flipped open the journal to reveal the coded gibberish contained within, along with the loose-leaf pages filled with my translations.

"I already told you. The journal only explains how they escaped the cult and their shared husband. It barely even mentions the fact that all three of them were pregnant. Lisianthus didn't seem to want to dwell on that fact too much, and mostly focused on the logistics of their escape. There's no mention of an underground vault anywhere."

Flipping to the back of the book, I turned to the very last page.

"The only page that stands out is this last one here."

All six of us leaned over the table, examining the last page from various angles.

To grow, to build, and to survive. The future lies in the strength of one's spine.

These were the exact same words I'd translated earlier. Nothing had changed. It provided no answers, and just sounded like a profound sendoff for an overall unpleasant story.

We all stared at the page and its meaningless words, until Trent suddenly picked up the journal and started turning it over in his hands.

"You know, when the police first asked me to look over the antiques they found in that coffin you guys dug up, I didn't get to take a very close look at them. I was mostly focused on the most obvious details, but now that I've gotten a closer look at the journal, I realize that the binding is off."

"Off?" Magnus questioned. He moved like he was going to take the journal from Trent and look for himself, but then changed his mind. "What do you mean, *off.*"

"Its hard to explain without going into a detailed lectured about how old books were bound, but the leather on the spine looks thicker than the rest of it. It should all be one piece of leather, and the spine usually gets stretched the most, so that shouldn't be the case."

Magnus, Brody, and I shared a look,

and we all seemed to come to the same conclusion at the exact same time. Without a word, Magnus took the journal from Trent and handed it over to Brody, who pulled out a knife and used it to split open the journal's leather binding.

Hidden within the spine of the book, we found three long, thin strips of leather. Each was printed with a series of random numbers, along with an engraving of a specific flower at the top.

Three strips of leather, each labeled with either a rose, a poppy, or a Lisianthus flower. It was clear that each one coordinated to one of the Milford sisters, but the numbers made no sense. Even when I tried using the code that Lisianthus had used for the rest of her journal, it was still meaningless.

"So, that's one more key to the puzzle," Ellis said as he examined one of the leather strips. "But what does this tell us?"

"Nothing," I said as I threw one of the other leather strips onto the table. "This tells us nothing. These sisters are driving me up the wall with their constant codes and puzzles. I'm starting to think they're doing it just to be annoying."

Kayden picked up the leather strip I'd just throw down. "Maybe not. Like you said, the sisters were interested in codes and stuff like that. I think... these leather strips might be a scytale."

He said it with such certainty, but I'd never heard that word before, and judging from the looks on everyone else's faces, neither had they.

"What's a scytale?"

"It's a method the ancient Greeks used to send coded messages," Kayden said, as though that should explain things.

We were all still just as lost.

With a sigh, Kayden picked up the wooden dowel. "Here. I'll show you. The message is printed out on a strip of leather, interspersed with other random letters, or in this case, numbers, to hide it. There's no way of knowing which numbers are part of the message, and which are meaningless, until you wrap it around a specifically sized dowel. Then, the numbers should line up."

As he spoke, he wrapped the leather strip around the dowel, keeping each new loop snuggly pressed against the one before it. In most places the numbers didn't line up, except for one specific place on the dowel where everything lined up perfectly. Assuming he was right, then the dozens of random numbers was actually a very specific string of eighteen numbers.

After doing this with all three pieces of leather, we started to see a pattern emerge. The numbers at the end of each series were almost the same, and after some debate, we realized these must be dates. They were the same year, near the beginning of the twentieth century, and no more than two months apart.

Right around the time when the Milford sisters had come to Emberwood.

My hand flew across a scrap piece of paper as I wrote the numbers down. "If we take out the dates, then we're left with twelve numbers."

"No," Brody disagreed as he pointed to a specific spot on one of the leather strips. "Twelve numbers and two decimals. See this spot here. It just looks like an imperfection of the leather, but it's too symmetrical. It must be intentional."

One could always trust Brody's sniper eyes to see what everyone else overlooked.

Adding the decimals to the string of numbers, I leaned back in my chair and looked at what I'd written down.

The answer was so obvious, I felt like an idiot for not seeing it before.

"It's latitude and longitude. These are records of an exact location and date."

CREED

Of course, our next step was to then look up those three locations.

At first, there was nothing special about those three locations, other than fact that they were all relatively nearby. We could have driven to any of them in just a few hours.

However, when we cross-referenced the locations with the dates listed as well, something surprising turned up.

"There used to be an orphanage at each of these locations," Magnus announced. "They're all gone now, but at the beginning of the century, each location was a sanctuary for orphan children."

Holding up his phone, he showed us an old black and white photo of a modest wooden building. Even in the picture, there was an eclectic mix of children sitting on the steps.

The answer was clear. No one needed to say it out loud as we looked at the picture. These orphanages were where the Milford sisters had dropped off their children before eventually making their way to Emberwood.

Trent toyed with the cut open leather of the journal, reexamining the spine where the leather strips had been tucked away.

"Why go through so much trouble just to hide that information?"

Surprisingly, it was Ellis who spoke up. The man usually preferred to say quiet and follow Brody's lead, so the sound of his voice filled with confidence, was extremely unusual.

"It's in the name. *Mothers of the Mountain.* They escaped from *The Tamed Souls* and dropped their children off at orphanages in order to protect them, so they wouldn't be dragged back into the cult. But they also couldn't bear to completely cut off all ties to their children. So, they kept this information recorded but hidden. That way no one would ever find out, but they could still hold onto the hope that they might be able to find their children again one day."

His conclusion was mostly speculation. There was no evidence that what he was saying was correct, and human motivation was always hard to predict.

Yet, some instinct in me said that Ellis was absolutely right.

"The information was still hidden until now," I couldn't help but point out. "That means they never were able to track down their children again. The entire population of Emberwood referred to them as mothers, but they spent their whole lives separated from their actual children."

They'd probably been waiting for a day when *The Tamed Souls* were no longer a threat to them, but despite living to an old age, that day never came.

As the six of us sat around, looking down at the remnants of the Milford sisters' final secret, we all silently mourned for these women who had lived over a century ago.

***

We got a call from Deputy Hillard a few days later.

Chester Grieve had died in custody.

The man was old, and the stress of having been arrested—as well as having his plans thwarted—had apparently been too much for him. He'd suffered a heart attack while in custody, and despite the efforts of several doctors, the man hadn't survived.

I couldn't say that I was saddened by this news at all. Chester Grieve had not only kidnapped me and Kayden but had also been behind all the shit that Brody and Magnus had gone through recently.

Good riddance.

With him gone, *The Tamed Souls* cult had no reason to continue coming after us. According to the investigation against them, most of the cult hadn't even known what Chester Grieve's ultimate goal was, and the few that did know weren't as convinced as he was that we actually were descendants of their founder.

When Chester Grieve died, the cult's motivation to pursue us died as well. Now, maybe we could finally sleep soundly at night.

At least, that was my hope.

A few hours after getting the call from Deputy Hillard, I sat on Brody's front porch, going over the blueprints for my own house. It would take a while. The foundation hadn't even been laid yet, but the future was finally looking bright, and it was the perfect time to continue moving forward.

Plus, I didn't want to live in the spare bedroom forever. Kayden and I needed our own privacy.

I would have been with Kayden right that moment, but he was busy talking to his editor trying to explain why he wouldn't have an article for her.

Trent and Ellis were also away. Trent had returned to look after his antique shop in town, and Ellis was continuing his job hunt. He had an interview at the local hardware store that looked promising. It wasn't glamorous work, but it would give him something to do while he figured out what he wanted to do.

Overall, it was a peaceful day.

That peace only lasted a few hours and was shattered when Magnus approached us with a guilty look in his eye.

"Hey, guys. Can I talk to you about something?"

Brody and I both looked up from the blueprint we'd been studying.

"What'd you do?" we said in unison.

"Nothing bad," he insisted. Although,

he then muttered under his breath, "At least, I don't think so."

Taking his own seat on the porch, he handed us each a file. Just from the weight of it, I could tell that it only held a few pieces of paper, but I had no clue what it might contain.

"So, I know we concluded that Chester Grieve was probably crazy, but I was curious, so I ran an ancestry test on myself."

"Please tell me you didn't use one of those commercial DNA tests," Brody said with a shake of his head. "Those things are public. We don't need some distant cousin you've never heard of knocking at our door."

Magnus quickly waved both hands in front of him, fending off Brody's accusation. "No, no. Nothing like that. I know someone who could run the test for me privately. Nothing will be public, but... well, look."

He held out his phone, which showed a long list of data. The first was the literal genetic breakdown of his DNA, but then under that was a complicated tree of various ancestors he was related to.

"What are we supposed to be looking at?" I asked. My gaze darted over the various lists of names and dates, but I found nothing out of the ordinary.

"Right there, at the end." Magnus pointed to the earliest name on one of the shorter branches of his ancestral tree. "Apparently, I have an ancestor who, at the turn of the twentieth century, grew up in an orphanage. I looked up the location of that orphanage and... it's the same location that Rose Milford allegedly dropped off her child."

This had to be a joke. I refused to believe it, but I also knew that Magnus wouldn't lie about something like this.

Surely, there had to be a mistake somewhere.

I was still reeling from this new piece of information when Magnus, unfortunately, continued.

"I also looked up you two as well. The results are in the files I gave you. It looks like—"

"Don't," I interrupted him. "Don't tell me what I think you're about to say. I really don't want to hear it."

"But," he started to say, but I cut him off again.

"Nope. I'm not listening to this. Chester Grieve was crazy, and that's all there is to it."

I handed back the file without opening it and left to take a walk to cool my head.

My denial only lasted as long as it took me to make a few laps around our property. Eventually, curiosity won, and I ended up looking at the file anyway.

There it was, written in black and white.

Chester Grieve had been right all

along. That didn't change the fact that the bastard was still crazy, but in this one instance the man's instincts had been right.

Magnus, Brody, and I had met completely by chance while serving in the military.

What were the odds that all three of us would turn out to be distantly related?

Even more, what were the odds that we would randomly choose to settle down on the same patch of land where our ancestors had lived?

It was such an impossible coincidence that it almost seemed... unnatural.

No, I was not about to start entertaining the thought of witches and fate and the supernatural. Everything that had happened was entirely natural. Just very, very, very unlikely.

Magnus seemed more open to the idea of supernatural influence, while Brody was still on the fence about the whole thing. We agreed to disagree on the matter and left it at that.

The one thing we did agree on, was the fact that we needed to keep this information secret. Trent, Ellis, and Kayden could be brought into the loop, but other than that, we wouldn't tell another living soul.

The Tamed Souls still existed, though its threat had mostly been declawed without Chester Grieve, and the *Mothers of the Mountain* still had believers in Emberwood. If it ever got out that we were actually descended from the founders of both cults, we would never know another moment's peace.

The truth of our ancestry was locked away in Brody's safe, and we tried to forget it as best as we could. Maybe someday we would build our own complex security measures to keep the information safely hidden, but for now we were happy to pretend that it didn't exist.

There were plenty of other things for us to worry about, and a future that we needed to build.

CHAPTER TWELVE

Kayden

IT TOOK ANOTHER two months after our escape from the cult to finish building Creed's house. Summer had given way to autumn, and the mountain trees had changed from brilliant green to a fiery patchwork of colors. In that time, I'd left for a few small trips to appease my editor, but I couldn't bear to stay away for long and always ended up coming right back. I'd never built a house before, or done any woodworking for that matter, but I helped where I could. There was always plenty of basic labor that needed to be taken care of.

Creed had also managed to find a job, and I knew that he felt better now that he was able to contribute financially. About two weeks after Creed and I were rescued, a group of campers went missing out on the mountain. Creed volunteered his services to help find the missing campers, and his skills ended up being invaluable to the rescue efforts.

Apparently, the campers' GPS had been broken and took them in the wrong direction. None of them had been skilled enough at reading the environment around them to realize they were off track until they started running low on supplies. They'd been so far from their intended destination that even the rescue team's scent hounds were having trouble locating them. Creed's knowledge of the area and ability to read the almost invisible signs and tracks left by the group ended up being invaluable, and the rescue team even admitted that without him, they might not have found the lost campers in time.

After that, word quickly spread, and soon Creed was getting requests to escort people on their camping trips, and even host survivalist camps where he taught people how to survive in the wilderness. The work suited him well and brought in decent money. Plus, the flexible schedule allowed him plenty of time to work on building his house.

Or maybe, based on how much time I spent there, I should call it *our* house.

Finally, after months of hard work, the house was finished. The six of us had a party to celebrate the completion of the last main structure on the property.

Magnus and Brody, as well as their partners, stayed up well into the night, drinking and talking around the outdoor firepit. However, Creed grabbed my wrists and dragged me inside early.

"Come here. I... I prepared something."

I'd seen the inside of his new house before, but I still looked around at everything with interest as we passed by. It was a modest structure. Creed hadn't wanted anything too elaborate, as he planned to spend a majority of his time outside, but it was also comfortable enough to ride out a long winter cooped up inside without going stir-crazy. Most of the rooms were on the first floor, with only the master bedroom on the second floor. This left plenty of space for an upstairs balcony, and also put distance between the master bedroom and the guest bedroom. Just in case anyone needed to stay over.

Upstairs, Creed slowly opened the door to the master bedroom. An uncharacteristic pink blush stained his cheeks, leaving me dying with curiosity about what was on the other side of the door.

What I found was a scene straight out of a romantic comedy. The room was mostly open concept, bathtub, shower, and fireplace all living together in harmony. Apparently, Creed's love of the outdoors meant that he didn't understand the need for unnecessary walls inside and had designed the space himself along with Brody's help.

It was an unusual bedroom, but I'd seen it before and no longer found it surprising.

What did shock me was that there were now rose petals everywhere. A bright cascade of crimson covered the bed, the floor in front of the fireplace, and there was even a floral river leading to the bathtub. He'd also illuminated the space with more candles than were probably safe, giving everything a soft, intimate glow.

"What's this all about?" I asked as I entered the room, my feet kicking up more rose petals with each step.

Creed picked up a bottle of champagne that had been sitting in a tub of ice and held it in his hands like he wasn't sure what to do with it.

"Well, it's partly to celebrate the completion of the house, but also, you're leaving soon, aren't you? Finally going to the Himalayas like your editor wanted. Since I'm not going to see you for a while, I wanted to do something special. Did I get it wrong?"

I raised an eyebrow at him. "Wrong?"

"Yeah." He brought the champagne over to the tub where two glasses were waiting. "All of my research implied that this is the kind of stuff that couples do."

"Creed," I gaped at him. "Were you... were you studying romance movies to figure out how to have a relationship?"

At first, he started to nod, staring more

at his feet than at me, but then he seemed to change his mind and shook his head. "I started off with romance movies, but most of them featured a straight couple, and I feared that may not apply to us. Luckily, the Internet had more detailed examples."

Sometimes, it honestly seemed like Creed spoke his own language. All the words he said made sense on their own, but putting them together required me to translate his meaning.

"Creed, were you..." I had to pause for a moment to keep myself from laughing. "Were you studying porn to figure out how to be gay?"

"Well, when you say it like that is sounds ridiculous," he muttered under his breath.

For one moment, the pout on his face nearly broke my control and caused me to laugh out loud. If I had, then the romantic atmosphere he'd tried so hard to create would have been ruined. So, I bit my tongue, kept my laughter under control, and planted a kiss on his lips instead.

"It's perfect," I said, and I meant it. "Now, I'm not sure what you had planned for tonight, but I see two glasses of champagne and an extra-large, jetted tub that are dying to be shared. How about we start there?"

It was a night of indulgence.

We lounged in the bath, trading kisses and sensual touches, until the water went cold and every bubble had popped. I felt so clean that I almost expected to squeak when I walked.

After we climbed out of the tub, we intended to head for the bed, but never made it. We were so caught up in kissing that we ended up just sprawling out on the floor in front of the fireplace.

The faux fur rug cushioned us from the hard floor and was just large enough to hold us both. I entirely forgot we weren't on a bed as Creed climbed on top of me, trailing kisses from my mouth down my neck and even farther still to the rest of my body.

"Your... studies have been... paying off," I gasped as his tongue swirled around one of my nipples. In just two months, the stoic yet shy man who could barely say the word "sex" had disappeared. In his place, was a man of confidence who seemed to know exactly what to do to get me going.

What kind of porn had he been watching?

"You've been so patient with me," Creed said as he moved over to lavish the same attention on my other nipple. "I want to make you feel good as well."

"You always make me feel good," I tried to say, but the words mushed together into one jumbled sound when he bit my nipple just hard enough to send an electric jolt of pleasure racing up my spine.

He seemed to understand what I meant to say anyway, because he smirked up at me before continuing his exploration down my body.

When he reached my cock, I eagerly spread my legs for him. His mouth was like nirvana against my heated flesh, but to my shock he didn't stay there long. Instead, he gripped my hip and urged me to turn over.

"There's something new I want to try."

At first, I wasn't sure what he intended, until his mouth latched onto the skin right above the swell of my ass and sucked until a bruise formed.

"Are... are you sure?"

He pressed more kisses along the small of my back.

"Absolutely. I want to try everything with you."

After I agreed, I expected him to

hesitate, but he charged forward with an eagerness I hadn't expected. Grabbing my ass in both hands, he buried his face against me. The feel of his tongue against the rim of my hole was surprisingly cool, and I jumped from the unexpected sensation.

Even my previous partners hadn't wanted to do this with me. I'd never thought I was missing much, but as Creed's tongue wormed its way inside me, I realized I'd been wrong.

So, so wrong.

The feeling of his mouth down there, hot breath panting against me and his tongue working me open, was so different from anything I'd experienced before. It was smaller than a finger but moved so unexpectedly that his tongue somehow seemed to be everywhere at once.

I moaned and buried my fingers into the rug. Every inch of my body felt so sensitive, I was already on the verge of coming.

Maybe I was the one drugged this time.

My hips rutted against the floor, leaving stains of precum matted into the carpet. I was a sweaty, mewling mess, but I didn't care. All I cared about was begging for more.

Creed obliged, and pushed his tongue even deeper inside me, searching out nerve endings I didn't even know I had.

My climax hit me so unexpectedly, I nearly blacked out. I didn't even have time to take a breath before I was locked in the jaws of ecstasy. Creed held me in place the whole time, and didn't let go until, with a final gasp, I collapsed boneless against the carpet.

My thoughts were nothing but gray noise. I couldn't have formed a sentence if I tried. Somewhere in the back of my mind, I felt him spreading my legs and positioning his hips against me, but I was too wrung out to react. I put up no resistance as he slid into me. His thrusts were hard and fast, causing me to gradually slide up the carpet each time he slammed into me. We'd ditched the condoms after the first month of our relationship, so there was nothing separating us. I could tell he was already close to his end as well.

Gripping onto the ruined carpet, I hung on for dear life until he finished.

He was behind me, so I couldn't see him, but I heard his gruff shout and felt the warmth flooding through me when he reached his end. Then, after pulling out of me, he collapsed onto the carpet as well and we just lay there catching our breath in the firelight.

It was nearly fifteen minutes before we felt strong enough to move. Then, after quickly cleaning up and throwing the rug into the laundry with the hope of saving it, we climbed into bed together. There was an unspoken agreement between us that our night wasn't over yet, but for the moment we were content to simply lie tangled together.

My head was pillowed on Creed's chest, and from this position I could see out the window. I had a perfect view of the rest of the property, and I could even see a bit of firelight where the others were still gathered around their celebratory bonfire.

It was such a peaceful night. In that moment, this little piece of property seemed like heaven.

"Hey, Creed," I spoke up when a question occurred to me. "Do you ever give any thought to my earlier suggestion, about naming this place?"

Creed's hand stroked through my hair.

"Actually, yes. I talked it over with Magnus and Brody, and we came up with a name."

Turning away from the sight out the window, I looked up at him instead.

The smile he gave me could have

turned winter into spring.

"We've decided to call our home Trinity Escape."

Dear Reader,

THANK YOU for reading the Rock Hard Mountain Men series.

If you enjoyed this taste of brawny, hairy alpha men who once lived to serve their country, and now strive for nothing more than a simple life with some peace and quiet—yet seem to attract action and mystery, and perhaps a little bit of man on man lovin' along the way, then please let me know.

You can simply return to the online retailer where you made your purchase and leave me a short review.

Your thoughts may just encourage other readers to try my books, and help me continue writing the characters we all adore and root for.

Even a few words would mean the world to me.

☺

~Love, Evie Riley

OTHER BOOKS BY EVIE

My action-filled, romantic suspense, and darker-themed books:

Rock Hard Mountain Men
Magnus
Brody
Creed

Ruthless Empire
Courting Danger
Chasing Danger
Kissing Danger

Federal Protection Agency
Mason
Rafe
Ryzen
Cooper
Noah
Damien
Sebastian

EVIE RILEY

Gabe
Logan

Smokejumpers
Hawke
Cyrus
Jase
Gage
Jackson
Xavier

From The Edge
Shattered
Runaway
Jaded
Rescue
Hidden
Tormented

Gray Vale Pack
His Fated Mate
His Wounded Warrior
His Healing Heart

My more romance-themed books:

Rock His World

Hollow Heart

Wild Stars

Grave Misgivings

Jasper Springs

Cade

Dawson

Drew

Grayson

Riley

Mitch

ABOUT THE AUTHOR

Evie Riley believes too much time spent at the beach is barely enough. She enjoys spending time puttering in the garden, cooking yummy things for her family, and has a quirky personality, described by her partner as ranging from cute to deadly, depending on her blood-chocolate levels.

Evie crafts steamy gay male romance filled with all the edgy angst, or dark and gritty romantic suspense where her men must overcome difficult obstacles and may find love along the way while dishing out their own brand of justice.

Evie spends her nights writing bad boys in love, and her days wrangling the sweet boys she loves.

EVIE RILEY

www.ingramcontent.com/pod-product-compliance
Lightning Source LLC
Chambersburg PA
CBHW070345170726
48291CB00001B/184